Stuck in camel form, Rudy loses all track of time while held in a small, exotic animal zoo run by a circle of witches. They even saddle him up and use him to give customers rides. When demons wipe out the witches and their acolytes, he's certain he and the other shifters in the place will be next. Instead, the demons free them and take them to a shifter gang deep in the Louisiana bayou.

When Rudy and the several others who still can't shift are ordered to hide from an arriving vehicle, they obey. Curious, he peeks through the trees and watches three figures emerge from a black SUV—two clearly federal agents and one not. As they disappear inside, the most wonderful aroma drifts across Rudy's senses, and he realizes one of the visitors is his mate. Rudy longs to rush in and discover who, but he forces himself to wait, knowing he should only reveal himself to his one and only.

To Rudy's great relief, the federal agents leave, and their scents don't interest him. Even in camel form, Rudy makes it known that the visiting human—Gary Badoga—is his mate. Upon learning that Gary's head has been filled with lies about shifters by witches, can Rudy figure out a way to connect when Gary seems afraid of his animal?

The unauthorized reproduction or distribution of this copyrighted work is illegal. Criminal copyright infringement, including infringement without monetary gain, is investigated by the FBI and is punishable by up to 5 years in federal prison and a fine of $250,000.

This book is a work of fiction. Names, characters, places, and incidents either are products of the author's imagination or are used fictitiously. Any resemblance to actual events or locales or persons, living or dead, is entirely coincidental.

Pursuit by Camelback
Copyright © 2022 Charlie Richards
ISBN: 978-1-4874-3616-2
Cover art by Angela Waters

All rights reserved. Except for use in any review, the reproduction or utilization of this work in whole or in part in any form by any electronic, mechanical or other means, now known or hereafter invented, is forbidden without the written permission of the publisher.

Published by eXtasy Books Inc

Look for us online at:
www.eXtasybooks.com

Pursuit by Camelback
Kontra's Menagerie 33

By

Charlie Richards

DEDICATION

One reason people resist change is because they focus on what they have to give up, rather than on what they will gain.
~Unknown

CHAPTER ONE

"I'm really sorry, guys," Alpha Kontra stated, his attention sliding between them all. "We have some feds coming with a friend of Evan's, so since you can't shift, yet, we're going to need you to hide amidst the trees." While the big alpha clearly scented of remorse, his expression turned wry. "Some of you would be a little hard to explain without specialized permits."

If Rudy could have chuckled while in camel form, he would have. Kontra's statement couldn't have been truer. In most states, permits were required to own exotic pets, and all five of them were classified as exotic in one way or another. The little group comprised of himself, a dromedary camel, as well as an African elephant, a gray wolf, a capybara, and a coral snake.

"As soon as they're gone," Kontra continued. "We'll let you know." With a grimace, the alpha added, "I hope to be able to get rid of them quickly."

Rudy bobbed his head once in acknowledgment, as did the others. Turning, he flicked his tail toward his haunch to knock away a pesky bug. Then he wandered between cypress trees, mindful of each step he took. Rudy had no desire to get stuck in a bog, and with his size, he knew he would sink fast.

On Rudy's right, he saw the African elephant doing the same, moving slowly and watching his step. He didn't know the other shifter's name—he didn't know any of their names—for they'd all been trapped in animal form for the length of their captivity. The capybara stayed close to the elephant's side, while the gray wolf bounded forward agilely, disappearing quickly. Rudy watched the coral snake slither up a tree branch and out of sight.

Damn witches. Lost nearly six years of my life to them.

Rudy hadn't realized how much time had passed until they'd been rescued. His days had run together, blurring from one to the next. He was fed, gawked at, and even forced to give rides to customers during certain hours of the day.

Having been there so long, Rudy had practically given up all hope of rescue. After all, he didn't have any family or herd that would be looking for him. He'd been on his own, a lone shifter, for almost eighty years before someone had run his pick-up off the road and tranquilized him.

Waking in his animal form, in a cage, Rudy had initially rebelled. The stun guns and shock sticks had adjusted his attitude pretty quickly. So had the spells the women cast, revealing that they were witches.

Then . . . the demons had come.

Rudy had never seen a demon before, but he'd heard stories . . . long ago. The winged creatures had swept through the place, dispatching the few witches who'd been there as well as the handful of acolytes working as guards and help. With the scent of blood on the wind, Rudy had been certain all the animals would be next, and he would end up being tossed in some unmarked grave with the rest of the coven's animals.

Except, that hadn't happened.

The demons had recognized that some of the animals were actually shifters. After a brief stint in the demon realm, which Rudy had found fascinating, the demons' leader — the Horseman of Death — had brought Rudy and the others to Alpha Kontra Belikov. Evidently, the alpha had had some experience with combating chemicals and spells meant to hold a shifter in their animal form. They'd had blood drawn, and the alpha explained that it was being sent to a wolf shifter pack who had doctors that could analyze it.

Currently, they were waiting for the results.

The rumble of an engine drew Rudy's attention. He'd never seen federal agents before, and his curiosity bloomed within him. Carefully, after a quick glance around confirmed that his body was well hidden, Rudy lifted his head high enough to see over a tree branch.

Rudy watched a large, non-descript SUV roll down the driveway, rocking a little as it hit a pot hole. The vehicle stopped ten feet before the large, aging Victorian home that was Alpha Kontra's current home base. From what Rudy had heard, the biker gang was semi-nomadic, and they had a few places set up around the country in areas that were close to friends.

Considering the gang drove motorcycles as their means of transportation, coupled with the fact that Rudy and several others couldn't shift, Alpha Kontra and his gang wouldn't be going anywhere any time soon. Fortunately, the owner of the home—Olson—was a human mated with a shifter, and he had welcomed the large crew. In return, the shifters were helping Olson fix up his old home.

As Rudy watched, the two front doors on the vehicle opened. A man appeared from the driver's side door, and a woman stepped from the passenger side. Both sported the signature black suit and sunglasses, and Rudy found himself a little disappointed.

Guess I should have expected it considering all the police shows I've seen.

The pair said something to each other, but Rudy was too far away to hear what it was. He was just about to turn away when the rear passenger door opened. Clearly tentative, a slightly plump man eased from the vehicle. The man adjusted his gold-rimmed glasses before smoothing his nice polo shirt over his rounded belly.

With a hand, the woman beckoned to the timid-looking man, who jolted and hurried forward. Then the trio started toward the front of the house. They'd just reached the porch when the front door opened.

Sam stared at the group before saying something too quiet for Rudy to hear, but he assumed it was a greeting of some sort. The big Texas longhorn shifter, who was the gang's beta, took a step backward, swinging the door wide. He waved a hand toward the inside of the home, clearly welcoming them.

The male agent led, his expression and the tension in his body betraying his distrust. The female agent seemed much more relaxed. The third human threaded his fingers together and peered into the house, seeming to be looking for something . . . or someone.

As they disappeared inside, Rudy began to turn away. He allowed his attention to drift toward the plants around him, wondering if any of them would taste good to his camel. Rudy had just decided to sample the leaves on a nearby bush when an earthy, masculine fragrance teased his nostrils.

The pleasant aroma lit up Rudy's senses, and he inhaled deeply. He let out a soft grunt of appreciation as he turned his head, searching for the source of the smell. The fragrance caused heat to simmer through his veins, warming him from the inside out. An aura of anticipation even flooded him.

Except, after Rudy inhaled once more, the scent dissipated.

Rudy grumbled irritably, turning his head this way and that, lifting and lowering it, but the smell was gone. Frustration unlike anything Rudy had ever experienced surged through him, and he stamped his foot in anger.

Turning his attention to the house, Rudy wished he had the ability to shift, so he could talk to Alpha Kontra about it. Perhaps he would be able to help him locate the source. After all, he'd already seen Kontra use Payson, a hyena shifter, as a hound dog to track a human through the swamp.

I bet that shifter could tell me what caused that amazing aroma.

I want to nuzzle against it and — Oh shit! Did I just scent my mate?

Once the idea hit Rudy's brain, everything clicked into place. It made sense. He'd caught a faint odor for a moment when the new people walked up to the house.

Oh, wow. One of them is my mate!

Rudy took two steps toward the house, eagerness filling him. Something gripped his hind leg and tugged lightly. Pausing, Rudy turned his head and saw the elephant had wrapped his powerful trunk around his limb.

The elephant eased his hold as he shook his head, silent questions filling his deep gray eyes.

Wishing again that he could shift, Rudy grumbled his frustration. He did still, however. He knew what the elephant was warning him about — the alpha wanted them to stay hidden.

Forcing himself to relax, Rudy bobbed his head once, accepting the elephant's warning. The larger beast cocked his head, obviously still wondering what was up with him. Rudy wished he could answer.

Instead, Rudy allowed his breath out in a rush of frustration, and he turned back to face the house.

Then . . . he waited, occasionally flicking his tail at a fly as he watched for the humans to appear again. He reminded himself over and over that Kontra would be able to give him information on who was inside. One way or another, he could figure out who his mate was.

Rudy shifted from foot to foot, his excitement building as he saw the front door open once more. The federal agents exited the old Victorian. While the man was frowning, clearly displeased about something, the woman was shaking her head and smirking at him.

Breathing deeply, Rudy hoped to catch a hint of their scents. He was pretty certain that his mate wasn't the woman — *please, don't let it be the woman* — but he couldn't dismiss her right away, yet, either. They'd both climbed into the vehicle and shut their doors before Rudy managed to parse out their smells.

Okay. Not them.

That meant his mate with the shorter, plump human.

Rudy's anticipation ramped up, and he stared at the once more closed door, waiting for him to appear. Except, he didn't. Instead, Rudy heard the engine rumble to life, and soon after, the federal agents drove away.

My mate is still in the house.

That knowledge filled Rudy with a rush of excitement. He once again started toward the Victorian. That time, when the rope-like sensation tightened on his leg, he knew what it was.

Grumbling, Rudy barely resisted attempting to yank free of the elephant's trunk. He obeyed the unspoken urging—*wait*. After all, they'd been ordered to stay hidden until one of Kontra's people gave them the all-clear.

Waiting had never been so difficult for Rudy.

Finally, Rudy spotted Mutegi—the gang's lead enforcer—heading toward the woods . . . and them.

Unable to wait a second longer, Rudy rushed forward, ignoring a low-hanging branch and the way his hump pushed a limb up so far it creaked, threatening to snap. He barely even registered it when the branch swung back down and popped him on the left flank. Instead, Rudy was too focused on rumbling his excitement to the warthog shifter crossing the yard.

Mutegi lifted one hand as he cocked his head. "You know I cannot understand," he rumbled deeply in his slight African accent. "What is wrong?"

Rudy practically pranced from foot to foot, trying to figure out how the hell to explain. He really just wanted to barge into the house and seek out the cute human. Struggling, he peered from Mutegi to the house and back again.

To Rudy's surprise, the elephant appeared at his side once more. He waffled softly, lowering the end of his trunk to the dirt. Rudy stared in surprise as he used his appendage to spell out a couple of words.

Mate here?

Pleasure and relief flooded Rudy in equal measure that someone had put the pieces together so swiftly.

Braying, Rudy bobbed his head in a semblance of a nod. He peered toward the house before refocusing on Mutegi. He even nudged the elephant's head before snuffling at the words written on the ground.

Mutegi's brows furrowed. "You believe Gary is your mate?"

Rudy's excitement mounted to have a name to go with the black-haired, bespeckled human's face. Still, he didn't know if Gary truly was his mate. Rudy needed to confirm it.

Prancing toward the house, Rudy grumbled excitedly.

Want to see my mate now!

Mutegi sighed deeply, but he did turn toward the house. His black eyes narrowed as he glanced from Rudy to the house and back again.

"As much as I hope Gary is your mate," Mutegi began, walking beside him. "You need to keep in mind that he has been lied to by witches." The big black male patted Rudy's shoulder as worry began to fill him, adding, "But you are one of us. We will help you in every way possible."

Rudy felt surprise and relief flood him as he realized that he once again had a herd, one that would watch his back, and that knowledge filled him with pleasure . . . and anticipation.

Now, if I could just bloody well shift.

CHAPTER TWO

Gary Badoga stared in shock at his best friend of nearly fifteen years. "I-I'm sorry," he whispered, barely able to get the words past his throat. "Wh-What did you just say?"

Disbelief flooded him.

Is this the same man who's been sharing information with me via the witch coven for the last year and a half?

"Shifters are not humans who have been infected with a virus," Evan repeated, his gaze steady upon Gary. "The witches lied to me . . . to us." Then he winced, and he lowered his gaze to the steaming mug of tea he rested upon his thigh. "And they lied about me being cursed. It really was me who hurt you. O-Or my magick, anyway, by accident." Peering at Gary through his lashes, Evan whispered, "I-I'm a warlock, and my powers were beginning to manifest, but I didn't know it."

Slowly shaking his head, Gary tried to muddle his way through that information dump. "U-Um, okay," he finally muttered, struggling. "Th-The witches were lying?" Squinting at Evan, Gary blurted out a few things of his own. "Why? Are you sure? How do you know? Who told you this?"

"Well." Evan paused and cleared his throat before taking a sip of his tea, obviously buying time. "Um, well . . . this is so hard to explain," he began, clearly uncomfortable. After heaving a sigh, Evan began rambling once more, "The doc and a lot of the others . . . well, they're shifters. The witches attacked them because these guys were helping the bears. Demons rescued them from the people the witches rented them to. They were treating them like property, even though they're a sentient species, and—"

"Whoa, whoa!" Gary cried, holding up one hand as he jumped to his feet. "Wait."

Gary shook his head as he stared down at Evan, shock flooding him as he tried to comprehend what he was telling him, but it was just too much. His buddy rested on a sofa, his leg up on the cushion. His friend had suffered from a cottonmouth bite while in the swamp . . . or so he'd told him on the phone. Evan had been missing for several days, and Gary hadn't been able to find him or the witches that he lived near, so Gary had filed a missing person's report.

After all, Evan was the brother Gary never had.

Odd things had begun to happen around Evan, but it wasn't until Gary had ended up injured with a broken leg that Evan had come clean. Gary had found information about a nearby wiccan circle online. As it had turned out, they'd been actual witches, and Amelia, the high priestess of the circle, had claimed Evan had been cursed.

"Back up." Gary waved his hands, inadvertently splashing some soda over his hand. Grimacing, he quickly put the can on the coffee table he'd been sitting on. "The witches lied?"

Evan nodded, nibbling his bottom lip.

"About what?" Gary needed specifics. "The curse?"

Evan had been living in an apartment over one of the witches' garages. He'd practically been their slave, doing whatever menial tasks they needed, since they were supposed to be helping him lift the curse he'd been under. Considering Gary had been the one to find and connect Evan with the witches, he would feel horrible if it had all been for naught.

"Please, Gary." Evan waved toward a chair to his right. "Sit down. I'm sorry I told you like that." With a sigh, he admitted, "It's just . . . there's so much to share."

Gary slowly nodded as he picked up his soda. After taking

a sip, he moved to the chair to the right of Evan. There was a small end table between the pieces of furniture, so Gary tucked his legs under him, cradled the can between his palms, and leaned his elbows on the arm of the chair.

"Okay." Gary blew out a breath as he faced his friend. "Let's try this again." He pointed one finger toward Evan's leg. "You were really bitten by a cottonmouth?"

Evan nodded. "Yes. I was bitten by a cottonmouth." Grimacing, he admitted, "Hurt like hell, but it's easing now." He pointed toward the archway where all the men had disappeared, obviously doing their best to give them space while they were in the front room of the old Victorian home. "Eli really is a doctor, and he gave me anti-venom. These guys really are a biker gang." Pinning a serious-looking gaze on Gary, Evan added, "And a lot of these guys are shifters." As Gary's jaw sagged open, Evan lifted a hand in placation and hurriedly stated, "That's one of the lies the witches have been telling us. Shifters are not humans infected with a virus that turns them into crazed, killer animals. Shifters are a completely different species."

"Oh my god," Gary whispered, his can beginning to shake due to the trembling of his hands. "But-but-but . . ." He snapped his mouth shut and shook his head before hissing, "Shouldn't we get out of here? They're dangerous!"

"We're perfectly safe here," Evan countered. His smile appeared so relaxed that Gary felt sure he believed what he claimed. Before Gary could think of a counter, Evan continued, "The only time the average shifter is aggressive is when they're defending themselves or their family." With a shrug, Evan added, "They're just like us, really. They want to live their lives, find love and happiness, maybe raise kids or something." His brows furrowing, Evan muttered, "I wonder if Shannon wants kids."

"Shannon?" Gary latched onto that, even glancing over his

shoulder as if expecting the large man who'd kissed Evan with passion before leaving the room to reappear. Rising onto his knees, Gary leaned partway across the end table as he whispered, "Does Shannon know about shifters?" Another thought hit Gary, and he could practically feel the blood draining from his face. "Is he . . . is *he* one?"

Gary gaped when Evan nodded, not appearing the least bit concerned. Shaking his head, Gary sat back. "But . . . but . . . he seemed so nice. Calm," he whispered.

The witches said that shapeshifters weren't calm.

But if they're not created by a virus, like the witches said, would anything they told him and Evan about shifters be real?

"Well, about that," Evan began slowly, his brows furrowing. "Only rogues are aggressive outside the whole protecting themselves thing I mentioned."

"Rogues?"

Nodding as he shrugged, Evan stated, "Every species has their bad apples."

"Right," Gary mumbled, nodding absently, his brain whirling. "Um . . . okay." Then he whispered, "So, Shannon is a shapeshifter, and you"—he blinked as he saw the small, happy smile curving Evan's lips—"you're obviously okay with that."

"Yeah."

"Wow," Gary whispered, uncertain what else to say.

Evan scoffed softly. "There's so much to explain. Like, they actually call themselves shifters, not shapeshifters, although I don't really know what the distinction is." He shrugged and shook his head. "And—"

"Anything else can wait for now." The man who'd been introduced as Kontra, the leader of the gang, strode into the room. "There's someone who'd like to meet Gary."

Although Kontra's huge frame intimidated the hell out of

Gary, the small smile curving his lips helped relax him. He eased back in his chair, clutching his can to his chest. "Um, okay."

"Relax, Gary," Kontra urged, settling in a large, wing-backed chair. "Nothing and no one will hurt you while you're here." Then he turned and called, "Bring him in, Mutegi."

A broad-shouldered man with skin dark as ebony strode into the room. His dozens of black braids fell around his shoulders as he glanced around the room, his gaze falling on Gary. He nodded once, then lifted a hand and beckoned.

Gary felt his brows shoot up his forehead when, instead of a man, a camel walked into the room. It immediately riveted its gaze upon Gary as it openly sniffed, its nostrils flaring. The beast's body almost appeared to vibrate as it stared at him.

"Gary is the one, camel?" Mutegi asked, which didn't make any sense to Gary.

What even confused him more was the way the camel dipped its head in an obvious nod before taking a couple of steps toward him.

"Easy, camel," Mutegi rumbled, placing his palm on the animal's shoulder. Then Mutegi focused on Evan. "Have you explained that we are sentient in animal form, yet?"

"Uh . . . no," Evan replied, glancing around the room at everyone. "What's going on?"

"The camel caught Gary's scent on the wind and found it entrancing," Kontra told them, as if that should be some kind of explanation. A smirk curving his goateed lips, he added, "I commend him for being able to stay away, even for the short duration of the federal agents' visit."

"You commend him for staying away," Evan repeated, sounding just as confused as Gary felt. Then Evan gasped and glanced between them. "Oh my god. Does that mean?"

The camel bobbed its head again before easing closer a few more steps.

Tensing, Gary leaned back in his seat. "Uh, why's it coming closer to me?" he couldn't help but ask. "Is it going to spit at me?"

Gary had heard somewhere that camels spat at those they didn't like.

To Gary's surprise, a clearly offended expression crossed the camel's features. It even grumbled a sound of annoyance. *Huh?*

Kontra snorted as he shook his head. "No, I'm pretty sure that he just told you, in no uncertain terms, that he won't spit at you." Smirking, he added, "He even seemed pretty offended that you'd even suggest it."

"H-He, uh . . . what?" Gary swiftly shook his head as something else clicked, and he muttered, "You've all been talking to it as if it can understand you."

"The camel isn't an *it*," Evan gently correctly. "The camel is a he. He's a shifter." Pointing at the animal, he added, "And, yes. He can understand us. A shifter is totally aware while they're in their animal form."

Snapping his attention to Evan, Gary gaped. "Wh-What?"

Evan offered him an understanding smile. "I know. Shocked me, too." His expression saddening, he murmured, "You remember me telling you about the cage with the bears? How I had to clean it? How scary it was for me, thinking I was in the same room as humans that had gone crazy from a virus?" Once Gary had nodded, Evan continued, "Imagine how horrible it was for Shannon and those bears? They were totally aware of everything going on around them, of what was being done to them, of what they were being forced to do by the witches because of their spells."

"Oh, god." Gary felt his stomach churn at the thought. He rubbed his soft belly, trying to ease it, before taking a quick sip of the soda. As Gary swallowed, he registered something Evan had said. "Wait. Shannon was one of those bears?"

Nodding, Evan explained, "Yeah, and he knew I was his

mate from the beginning, but the spells binding him meant he couldn't do a thing about it."

Gary rubbed his face with one palm, his mind reeling with all the new information being thrown at him. All he'd planned to do was make certain his bestie was safe . . . and maybe take him home. Instead, Gary felt as if he'd fallen down the rabbit hole.

"Wait." Gary snapped his attention back to those in the room. While he'd been thinking, he realized the camel had eased several steps closer. In fact, the beast — shifter — was almost within touching distance, and he cringed away, fear creeping through him. "Um, why does it . . . um . . . *he* keep coming closer to me?"

"Because," Kontra answered. "You are the camel's mate." Before Gary could again ask what that meant, the big man continued, "The mate of a shifter is . . . the love of his life. His soul mate. The other half of his soul. The person he's been searching his whole life to find." Kontra's goateed lips curved into a smile that looked pleased for them both. "Once the camel can shift to human form, you'll have a lot to talk about."

"Y-You make it sound like, um, sound like" — Gary was having a hard time wrapping his brain around what Kontra was saying, but he forced himself to finish — "um, like we're going to be a, uh, couple."

Evan chuckled as he waggled his eyebrows. "Yup. That's exactly right."

Gaping at his friend, Gary barked, "No fucking way."

CHAPTER THREE

Unable to help himself, Rudy flinched. Never in a million years had he guessed that his mate would respond quite like that after the mate revelation. Fear slithered through him that his mate was rejecting him out of hand.

"Easy, camel," Kontra rumbled, rising from his seat. "I'm sure Gary didn't mean it quite like it sounded." He settled his hand on Rudy's neck and rubbed lightly. "I'm sure Gary is just surprised. That's all." Turning his attention to Evan, Kontra asked, "What do you think?"

Evan opened his mouth, closed it again, then opened it to say, "Absolutely. There's still so much explaining to do." His smile appeared a little uncertain as he asked, "Since you're standing in the house in camel form, I'm guessing you can't shift, yet, huh?"

Rudy shook his head slowly, frustration welling up within him.

"I will put in a call to Lark. Perhaps he has news on your bloodwork," Mutegi stated, heading out of the room. "And I will send in some of the human mates. They seem to be able to explain it best."

"So glad you called for us." Payson came strutting into the room, Land on his arm. "Always happy to help."

"You are *not* human," Mutegi muttered with a shake of his head and a roll of his black eyes even as he continued out of the room.

Payson blew a raspberry at the larger shifter's back before saying, "But my mate is." Then he claimed the wing-backed chair Kontra had been using, pulling Land onto his lap. "Hey, we should totally get some refreshments," Payson claimed. "This cool shit is best discussed over fatty comfort foods and alcohol." Grinning, he asked, "Gary, what's your pleasure?" With a snicker, Payson continued, "Sorry, camel, I don't think you should get any beer, although a drunken camel might be fun to watch."

Rudy grumbled irritably, thinking a beer sounded damn good. Although, truthfully, he had no desire to drink one as a camel. He just needed to shift.

Once again, Rudy reached for his human form. He pictured hands and feet, arms to hold his mate, and his body shuddered. Just when he felt confident he'd managed to start his shift, pain speared through his head, making his vision swim. His legs buckled, and he crashed to the floor hard, causing the floor to shake.

Frustration and anger surged through Rudy, and he groaned, resting his muzzle on the cool wood floor as he tried to catch his breath.

"Hey, hey," Kontra soothed, kneeling beside him. "Don't try to force it and hurt yourself, camel." Evidently, the alpha had realized exactly what Rudy had been trying to do. The big grizzly shifter moved his hand up and began massaging the poll of his neck, right behind his ears. "You're not alone, camel. We'll figure this out."

Grunting in acknowledgment, Rudy breathed deeply for a few minutes. When his head no longer threatened to pound off his shoulders, he looked up and saw Gary staring at him. To his relief—and surprise—Rudy felt certain he saw concern in the man's pretty pale-green eyes.

"What happened?" Gary asked softly, furrowing his brows. "It, um . . . is he okay?"

Rudy appreciated that Gary seemed to be trying.

Kontra sighed deeply as he rose to his feet. "The circle of

witches that you and Evan knew, well, they weren't the only ones capturing and exploiting shifters." He indicated Rudy while moving to a new chair. "We can't find any evidence of spells forcing them to stay in animal form, like the Crescent Moon Circle used on the bear shifters, so we're guessing they went the chemical route."

"Chemical route?" Gary parroted, telling Rudy that the man was probably on mental overload.

Learning about shifters can do that to humans, or so I've heard.

Once again, Rudy wished desperately for arms, so he could hold his mate, to soothe him.

To Rudy's shock, he felt his legs twitch and his skin ripple. Once more, pain burned through his system. That time, however, he did his best to ignore it as he reached for his human form once more.

Rudy felt the change begin even as it felt as if his body was being flayed by fire from the inside out. Shudders racked him, far more intense than anything caused by a normal shift. Doing his best to push through it, Rudy thought of his mate, of running his fingers through his hair, of kissing his full lips, and of caressing his soft-looking skin.

By the time Rudy's head reshaped, black spots danced across his vision, and he could barely stay conscious. Only needing to know he'd done it, he'd returned to human form, plus the knowledge that his mate waited, kept him focused enough to stay lucid.

When Rudy finally began processing again, he felt a hand rubbing up and down his bare back. There was something warm draped across his butt and legs. The cold of the floor soaked into his front, and it felt so soothing against his overheated, sweaty flesh.

"You with us, man?" Kontra rumbled, and Rudy realized it was the alpha once again kneeling beside him.

Damn. When was the last time you saw an alpha helping a herd member like this?

Rudy couldn't think of one time . . . ever.

After Kontra questioned him again, Rudy realized he needed to answer the man.

Except, when Rudy opened his mouth, his throat was dry and hurt so very badly. "W-Water," he croaked roughly.

"Here."

Rudy recognized the voice as Sam, a small submissive wolf shifter mated to Eli, the gang's doctor. Feeling the straw prod at his lips, he accepted it gratefully. Swallowing the first mouthful of cool water hurt, and he realized he must have been screaming as he shifted. Fortunately, the more Rudy drank, the better he felt, and Sam didn't pull the straw away.

After Rudy stopped drinking, he used his tongue to push the straw from his mouth. He tried to peel open his eyelids, surprised to find them gummy. Rudy realized he might have been crying, too.

Shit. What a horrible first impression to make with my mate.

"Just lie still and catch your breath, buddy," Kontra urged, massaging the back of his neck lightly.

"I'm going to draw blood, camel shifter," Eli stated, revealing he was there, too. "Keep relaxed. I want to find out if there are differences to what we drew last week."

"Okay," Rudy muttered, too tired to worry about that. Lethargy rolled through him, and he struggled to stay awake. Only the need to see Gary, to see how he was taking the change, kept him from passing out.

The pinch of the needle barely registered, hardly painful at all after the agony of his first shift in . . . nearly six years.

A moment later, Eli told him, "Okay. I'm done. Just stay down until the trembles in your limbs recede. I can still see them twitching."

Rudy nodded, feeling what Eli referred to. He couldn't remember the last time he'd felt so weak.

"Are you okay with me giving you a sponge bath?" Sam asked softly, his warm breath ghosting over Rudy's ear.

As much as Rudy would have preferred a shower, he couldn't even guess how long it would take for strength to return to his limbs.

"After that, Kontra can move you to a sofa so you can sit and talk to your mate," Sam added, as if Rudy needed a little incentive. "I think Yuma and Hunter are getting a couple of the guys together," Sam continued. "They're going to put together a meal, and, hopefully, it won't be too difficult for you to eat."

Hearing his stomach rumble, Rudy offered a soft chuckle. "Sounds good."

I'll figure it out. I'm hungry.

With his permission, Sam began rubbing a warm, damp cloth over Rudy's back, wiping away the sweat from the most painful shift of his life.

Rudy hesitated a few seconds, then forced his head to tip a little to the side. Ignoring Sam's ministrations, Rudy sought out Gary. "Hi," he mumbled once he met his mate's wide green eyes. Rudy forced a smile, hoping it didn't appear too tremulous, as he added, "I'm Rudy. Thank you, Gary."

Gary blinked a couple of times, his expression a range of confusion, disbelief, and even uncertainty. "I, uh . . . wh-why?" His black brows drew together to be partly hidden by the gold rims of his glasses. "Why are you thanking me?"

Rudy continued to stare at Gary, admiring his handsome features. As much as he wished he had the strength to slide his fingertips over the human's flushed cheeks, he knew he didn't. Contenting himself with just staring, Rudy formulated his response.

"I've been trapped in my camel form for nearly six years," Rudy explained, rubbing his fingertips over the hardwood floor in anticipation of touching his mate. "The demons rescued me a couple of weeks ago, and I still hadn't been able to shift. Every time I tried, there was so much pain."

"I-I don't blame you," Gary whispered. "With the way you

s-screamed." Hunching his shoulders, he shuddered. "If shifting like that hurt so much, I wouldn't want to do it, either."

"That's just it," Rudy replied. "It doesn't normally hurt like that. It normally feels pretty good, like a really great stretch after working out or just waking up. A fantastic warm muscle burn," he told Gary, doing his best to explain when his mate's features took on a disbelieving look. "But the chemicals making me unable to take on my human form must have been wearing off. I could feel my human form, but I couldn't achieve the shift due to pain." Smiling warmly at Gary, Rudy told him, "You gave me a reason to push through that pain."

"Wh-Why?" Gary asked again, obviously still struggling to believe.

Rudy sighed softly before stating, "You are my mate, Gary. I would endure anything for you." Not wanting to hear a denial from his human, he hurried to add, "When my strength returns, I hope to have the chance to hold you. To kiss you. But for now, I just wish to talk to you, to learn everything about you."

Feeling Sam move the blanket off his legs and begin working his way up, Rudy returned his attention to the small wolf shifter. "I think that's good for now," he stated. No way was he allowing the other male to wipe any higher than his thighs.

Sam smirked while rolling his eyes. "I know what you're thinking, and I'm a nurse by profession, so I've done it before." Then he indicated the room full of people. "But I understand your reticence, considering the audience." As Sam spoke, he picked up a dry cloth and dipped it into a bowl of water. After wringing it, he held it out to Rudy. "Here. You can do your face yourself, then the alpha or someone else can move you."

Rudy took the cloth, not surprised when his hand trembled a little and his fingers felt stiff and weak. Still, he managed to wipe his face and neck himself. Once he'd given the cloth back to Sam, Rudy remained impassive as Kontra knelt beside him once more.

"All right then," Kontra rumbled as he eased his arms under Rudy's pliant, tired body. "Let's get you situated on that sofa near the fireplace." Lifting him, Kontra smiled at Gary as he moved past him. "Maybe you'd like to move over here, too, so the pair of you can eat and talk. We'll keep explaining things, hmm?"

As Kontra placed him on the indicated small sofa, tucking the blanket around his hips, Rudy watched with bated breath, hoping, waiting to see if Gary would join him.

Chapter Four

Gary stared as Kontra carried Rudy to the sofa and settled him there. Indecision filled him. He couldn't deny that he found the man super sexy, with his shaggy, dirty-blond hair and wiry, muscular body. His fingers twitched where Gary once again had them wrapped around his now-empty soda can. Rudy's chest muscles and six-pack abs practically called for his touch.

As much as Gary wanted the opportunity to explore Rudy, who he knew would clearly welcome his attention, he didn't know if he wanted to perpetuate their belief in predestined soul mates.

That couldn't really be a thing, right?

Feeling a poke to his arm, Gary turned his attention to Evan. His friend offered him an encouraging smile. Then he made a shooing gesture with his hand.

Okay. Evan clearly thinks this is real.

Wait a minute.

"So, Shannon is *your* mate?" Gary mumbled the question, although he really already knew the answer. As his buddy nodded, smiling widely, he asked, "How are you okay with this idea of someone else, uh, Fate, choosing who you should end up with?"

Gary just didn't get it.

Evan scoffed as he shook his head. "How is that any different than using an online date matching service?" he asked with a shrug, reminding Gary that he'd created profiles on a couple of different sites. "You fill out a profile with your likes, dislikes, preferences, and such. Then the system lines you up with possible matches. Same thing, really."

"Yeah, but I still get to decide who I talk to or meet for a date," Gary pointed out. "This? This isn't anything like that." He turned his attention to Rudy, and found he really disliked the expression on the man's face. *Hurt? Or worried?* Needing to reassure Rudy somehow, Gary stated, "I'm sure you're a nice guy and all, but why would you just accept this? You don't know anything about me. What if we can't stand each other?"

"I've seen Fate bring a lot of couples together over the years, Gary," Kontra cut in, crossing his arms over his barrel chest while leaning against the wall. "And each time, their strengths and weaknesses complemented each other. That's not to say it doesn't take work," the big man added. "Any relationship is work. All Fate does is let the shifter know that the work will be more than worth it."

"You've signed up with dating sites?" Rudy asked softly, his deep voice still sounding a little hoarse. Sam handed him a cup of water, and Rudy murmured, "Thanks."

"Um, yeah," Gary admitted.

"So, you're open to a relationship." Rudy offered a crooked grin. "Consider Fate a relationship app." With a shrug, he tipped his chin toward the seat next to him. "And we're just talking, right now." Rudy scoffed softly, admitting, "It's the only thing I have energy for, Gary, and I'd never force myself on you. I want my mate willing, eager even, for my attentions." He hesitated a second, then added, "When the time comes for that."

"Put like that," Gary whispered. "Okay."

Gary took a deep breath before easing to his feet. He did want a relationship. He wanted someone to care for him and only him.

Why am I fighting this? Gary wasn't entirely certain as he made his way to the sofa. *Is it because he's a shifter, and for so long, I thought they were evil?*

As Gary gingerly settled next to Rudy, he wondered if he was truly that prejudiced . . . or stuck in his ways that he couldn't change.

"Thank you, Gary," Rudy rumbled softly, smiling at him. He stared at him, warmth filling his deep amber eyes . . . eyes the same color as the camel's. "I appreciate you giving us a chance to talk. I know you've had a hell of a lot of shocks today."

Gary nodded. "Yeah." Snapping his mouth shut, he wondered what else to say.

"Hey, guys." A slender man with black hair and frosted white tips strolled into the room. "Sorry that took so long. We had to change the propane tank on the grill." With a laugh, he added, "Me and Hunter had never had to do that before, so we ended up having to find Olson to show us how." The guy set the massive platter he carried on the coffee table before straightening and grinning at Gary and Rudy. "Hey, Gary. I'm Yuma, by the way." Touching his chest, he added, "Penguin shifter. This is Hunter."

Yuma indicated the brown-haired man who'd followed him into the room. The man was busy placing a tray filled with assorted beverage choices next to the one Yuma had set down. Hunter glanced up and smiled at the introduction before picking up a corkscrew and a bottle of wine.

"Hunter is human, too," Yuma continued with a grin. "We have a good mix here, so you two won't be the lone humans." He glanced at Evan and winked, clearly meaning the comment for him, too. Finally, Yuma rested his hands on his slender hips and cocked his head. "So, you're the camel. Congrats on finally shifting as well as meeting your mate. Mutegi told us. What's your name?"

Gary just stared in surprise as the obviously happy — and chatty — man rattled through all that. His excitement for them was a damn near palpable thing. Yuma even bounced on his toes a little as he grinned broadly at them.

"Hi, Yuma. I'm Rudy," the man next to him replied with a smile. "And thank you. I feel truly blessed by Fate." He turned his smile on Gary and murmured, "After fearing I'd die in that exotic animal zoo, I'm overjoyed that she has not forgotten me."

"You were in a zoo?" Gary frowned. "Right. Kontra told me that."

Yuma plucked Gary's empty can from his hands, grinning broadly at him. "So, what would you like to drink?" he asked, turning back to the coffee table and setting down the can before he began ticking off options on his fingers. "Beer, wine, water, tea, coffee, a variety of juices and sodas." Then Yuma grinned at Evan. "Sorry, Evan. You're still recovering. No alcohol or caffeine for you."

Evan sighed deeply, giving an exaggerated eye roll. "I know," he quipped forlornly.

"You'll be okay soon, baby," Shannon assured as he strode into the room carrying another tray, this one containing plates, utensils, and more food. After he placed that on the sideboard, he moved to Evan's side. He bent and placed a slow sipping kiss on Gary's friend's lips, which Evan welcomed eagerly.

Feeling his cheeks heat upon watching the open display of affection, Gary turned his attention to his hands. He threaded his fingers together and thought about Yuma's question. "A, um, a glass of red wine, please?"

"Sure thing," Yuma replied bubbly. "And you, Rudy?" Then his black brows furrowed. "Oh, maybe I better ask the doc." He turned his attention to Eli. "Doc?"

Eli offered a wry smile. "Rudy can have whatever he wants."

Yuma nodded before grinning at Rudy once more.

"Whatever dark beer you have would be fantastic," Rudy told him. Then he focused on Gary. "So, Gary. How'd you end up coming here?"

Gary took the glass of wine from Yuma as he shared how Evan had ended up missing, and he'd made a missing person's report. When Evan had called Gary, he hadn't been certain he believed his story about being bit by a snake. He was worried that his best friend was being held against his will, so he'd gotten the feds involved.

"And so, Evan convinced me to stay, telling me we'd hang out and have a little vacation together while he recovers." Gary took a sip of his wine as he pinned his buddy with a narrow-eyed stare. "Of course, then he blows my mind by starting to talk about shifters and how the witches lied to us." Lowering his wine glass, Gary asked, "Hey, didn't you say something about you being a warlock or something?"

Evan grinned from where he was cuddled up in Shannon's arms. The big man had eased behind his friend on the sofa, spreading his legs. Now Shannon was cradling Evan, his chest to his friend's back, while nuzzling his lips over Evan's neck.

"Yep," Evan replied with a chuckle. "There are two warlocks here, and they're going to teach me." He sobered and added, "That way I won't keep having weird things happen."

"Then, why did the witches keep you around?" Gary asked, frowning. "And what was that monthly ritual they were doing to you?"

"They were draining my magick so they could boost their own." Evan shivered a little, and Shannon made soothing noises as he caressed Evan's sides. "Evidently, if they'd taken too much, they could have killed me, but they wanted me alive. Kinda like a living battery."

"Bitches!" Gary hissed, vindictiveness flooding him. "Please tell me they're dead."

"I couldn't say," Kontra revealed as he grabbed a beer off the coffee table. "They were taken by a couple of the Horsemen of the Apocalypse. They're dealing with the rogue witch circles, since they'd been killing their demons to harvest their blood for spells." The big man's lips curved into a hard smile as he popped the cap off the bottle, and he chuckled darkly. "My vote would definitely have been death for them all, but I think they intend to interrogate them first. They'll wish they were dead."

A shiver went through Gary, and he hoped he never ended up on the shifter alpha's bad side.

"You're okay," Rudy whispered, reaching over and gripping Gary's free hand. Gently, he threaded their fingers together. "He's not upset at you."

Gary peered at Rudy, seeing his encouraging smile. His heart sped up as he stared at the other man's lips. They were smooth and full, and he couldn't help but wonder what the man tasted like.

Rudy chuckled softly as he brought his free hand up to Gary's face. Gently, he cradled his jaw. "I see the way you're looking at me," he murmured, his hazel eyes darkening almost to brown. "And I would love to taste your lips." Then Rudy winced a little as he admitted, "But it's been a hella long time since I've had the opportunity to brush. You mind if I do that first?" The shifter's stomach grumbled loud enough for Gary to hear it, and Rudy smirked. "After a meal?"

Realizing where his mind had strayed to, Gary quickly nodded. He turned his head, breaking contact with Rudy's gaze, and took a quick sip of wine. "Um, yeah. Yeah, we should eat, and um, keep talking." Gary felt his face heat for a new reason as embarrassment swelled within him.

"Hey, none of that," Rudy murmured, squeezing the hand he still held. "I'm not upset. I'm flattered, and I love that you respond to me." After clearing his throat, Rudy admitted,

"And I'm hard as nails under this blanket, and it sucks, because I really don't have the strength to do anything about it."

Gary couldn't help it. He lowered his gaze to Rudy's groin. Except, due to the way the blanket was bunched up around his waist, even his navel was barely visible.

"Let's eat, my mate," Rudy encouraged roughly. "And talk." Squeezing his hand once more, he asked, "So, where do you call home?"

Hearing the clink of dishes and murmurs of others talking, Gary yanked his head out of the gutter. He'd never been so brazen in his life. He wondered if what he was feeling was partly caused by Rudy claiming he was his mate.

Meeting Rudy's intense gaze once more, Gary answered. "A small town in southern Tennessee."

Chapter Five

As much as Rudy loved how Gary had been staring at him, betraying his attraction with his attention as blatantly as from his scent of arousal, Rudy knew he couldn't do a damn thing about it, yet. His arm still trembled just a little from when he'd lifted it to Gary's face. Rudy couldn't believe how much that first shift had taken out of him.

With that in mind, Rudy released Gary's hand, so he could take the bottle of beer Hunter offered and the plate Yuma held. "Are you strong enough to lift a burger?" the penguin shifter teased.

Rudy eyed the bacon cheeseburger and hummed. "Oh, yeah. No problem," he assured, setting the plate on his lap. Then he took a sip of his beer, appreciating the dark, hoppy flavor. "Gods, that's good. Been way too long."

"So, how did the witches capture you?" Gary furrowed his brows and added, "Is it okay to ask that?"

"You may ask me anything, my mate," Rudy told him. "I have no idea how they pegged me as a shifter," he admitted as he carefully picked up his burger. "I didn't recognize any of those who attended me at the zoo." Rudy still had no idea how he'd been targeted. "I'm an electrician . . . or I was," he amended. "I was on my way home from a job when someone rammed into my truck. I was forced off the road and hit a tree." With a shrug, Rudy finished, "I had just managed to shove open my door and slide from my truck when a dart hit me in the thigh. After that, I woke up in a zoo enclosure, and

I couldn't shift." He glanced around, realizing he had the attention of everyone in the room. "That was nearly six years ago." Rudy met Kontra's gaze. "Thank you for taking me in. I'm certain the sentiment is the same from the other guys, too."

Finally, Rudy took a big bite of his burger. He let out a soft moan as the flavor of the cooked meat and toppings burst across his taste buds. If he'd had as good a burger before his captivity, he couldn't recall when.

"You're welcome," Kontra replied with a grin. "I can only imagine how good that first food and drink is after so long." With a chuckle, he added, "We'll pester you with questions another time."

Rudy appreciated that as he swallowed the delicious food and quickly took another bite.

For the next few minutes, very little talking commenced. Instead, they focused on their food. Others came and left the room, introducing themselves while fixing a plate. Rudy just smiled and nodded at each, barely saying more than his name.

Once the meal was winding down, Kontra asked, "So, you said you were an electrician?"

Nodding, Rudy confirmed, "For about the last eighty years. My last three identities in various states."

"Glad to hear it." Kontra smirked as he chuckled softly. "Me and the guys are good at a lot of things, but none of us are much when it comes to electrical." Grinning, he told him, "Olson needs the wiring in this place checked. Lamar found some videos online, and Ben and Mutegi have been studying them, but it'd be nice to have a professional handle it. When you're up and around, think you can get started on that?"

"Of course, Alpha," Rudy immediately replied. "Uh, I'll need tools." Feeling heat threaten to bloom up his neck, he fought it back. "I have no idea what happened to my truck, house." He grimaced. "Anything, really. Hell, I may have been pronounced dead by this time."

"What was your last identity, and where were you located?" Lamar asked from where he'd been leaning against the wall. His mate, Rueben, stood next to him, an arm looped around his waist. "I'll look into what happened to your supposed self." The slender male smirked while adding, "I'll also get a new identity started for you. Have a preference on your surname?"

"Uh, I usually just use things like Brown and Johnson and stuff," Rudy admitted. "Nothing too exciting."

After Rudy had shared his prior surname — Smith — and where he'd been living in Connecticut, Lamar nodded, and he and his mate left.

"And don't worry, Rudy," Kontra added. "Just let us know whatever tools you need, and we'll get them for you."

As Rudy nodded, a jaw-cracking yawn overtook him. He lifted a hand to his mouth, covering it, as tears threatened at the corners of his eyes. Between the good food and the soothing scent of his mate, fatigue was creeping up on Rudy fast.

"You know," Evan commented, eyeing him. "Massage is supposed to be really good for helping circulation for strained or weak muscles." Curving his lips into a sly smile, he might have been going for an innocent tone when he stated, "You took that massage class in college, Gary. You remember much of it?"

Spotting the pink blooming on Gary's cheeks as his mate stuttered, "Um, y-yeah," Rudy reached over and touched the back of his human's hand.

"Don't feel obligated, my mate," Rudy told him. "I'm sure it's nothing that a good night's rest won't cure."

At least, Rudy sure hoped so. Feeling weak from shifting completely sucked.

"Um, n-no." Gary shook his head, and his smile appeared

a little uncertain. "I don't mind helping you."

"And massage is great foreplay," Payson piped up, grinning broadly. He waggled his eyebrows as he pinned a hungry gaze on his mate. "Isn't it, Land?"

Land's nostrils flared as a pinkish hue lit up his pale cheeks. "Oh, yeah."

Spotting even more pink infusing Gary's cheeks and neck, Rudy did his best to quickly reassure his mate. "But that wouldn't be the reason for you giving me a massage," he stated. "I don't expect a *happy ending*." Rudy lifted his fingers and made air quotes.

Gary's face turned an even darker shade as he muttered, "Okay." Then his brows furrowed, and he cleared his throat. "So, um . . . what did you mean by being an electrician for eighty years?" Gary swept his gaze over Rudy, his confusion apparent. "You can't be more than . . . what? Thirty-five?"

"Ah, we have gotten a bit distracted, haven't we," Kontra stated with a nod. "There's a few more bits to explain to your mate. While we do that"—Kontra peered toward Grimes, a lion shifter, and his bobcat shifter mate, Chip—"will you get a room set up for Rudy and Gary?" Then his brows furrowed. "Well, rooms, I suppose. That was a bit presumptuous of me."

Payson raised his hand. "Taking bets on whether or not Gary will actually use whatever room you set up for him."

Grimes chuckled as he headed from the room, his fingers threaded with Chip's as the much smaller male accompanied him. "We'll take care of it," Grimes assured as he disappeared.

"Well, then." Kontra returned his focus to Gary. "A few more things about shifters, mating, and how it all works."

For the next little while, the guys began sharing more information with Gary, whose scent varied from shock to confusion to disbelief and back again.

Rudy did his best to fight his fatigue, but he ended up resting his head on the back of the sofa. While he continued to hold Gary's hand, he couldn't keep his eyes open. Dozing, Rudy barely made out most of the guys' words, but he sure enjoyed listening to his mate's melodious tenor each time he asked a question.

Finally, Rudy felt a hand shake his shoulder. He peeled open his eyes and stared drowsily at Kontra.

"Let's get you upstairs, Rudy," Kontra urged. "Want me to carry you again? Or do you think you can make it?"

Rudy groaned as he leaned forward. "Wanna try to stand on my own two feet," he mumbled, rubbing his face with his palms.

"Okay." Kontra took a step backward, giving him room.

Carefully, Rudy gripped the arm of the sofa and used it as leverage to gain his feet. He straightened and swayed a little, clutching the blanket with his other hand. When Kontra grabbed his upper arm, Rudy nodded appreciatively.

"Grimes, show Rudy and Gary to their rooms," Kontra ordered.

Rudy didn't know when the black-haired man had returned, but the lion shifter nodded dutifully. "Come on, man." He grinned as he moved close, obviously ready to catch Rudy, just in case. "I have you in the first door on the left. It's not too far."

"Okay." Rudy took one slow step at a time, heading out of the room. He realized Gary wasn't following, and he paused to look behind him.

Gary stood beside the sofa, looking more than a little uncertain.

Evan patted Gary's hand and told him, "Go on, bestie. I'll see you in the morning."

"I didn't bring any clothes, though," Gary admitted, although he did take a step toward Rudy.

Yuma bounced up from where he'd been sitting on Hunter's lap. "I'm on it," he assured. "I'll find you a few things and bring them to you." Then the penguin shifter hustled away, adding, "And something for you, too, Rudy."

"Thank you, Yuma," Rudy replied, but the guy had already disappeared. As he followed Grimes to the staircase, he kept part of his attention on his mate. "I won't hold you to that massage if you don't want to, Gary." Smiling slightly, Rudy admitted, "I'm probably going to pass out really quickly."

"Um, I don't mind," Gary told him, although his scent gave away his uncertainty. "If I can help, then I want to." Frowning, he quickly added, "I mean, if someone has some kind of oil or something that they don't mind me using."

"Gotcha covered," Payson claimed, rising while placing Land on his feet, since his mate had been sitting on his lap. "You want flavored or unscented?"

"Unscented," Rudy quickly replied. He didn't want anything to obstruct Gary's delicious aroma.

Payson snickered, as if he knew exactly what Rudy had been thinking, and he hurried deeper into the house.

Rudy returned his attention to climbing the stairs. When he reached the top, he panted softly, and his legs trembled. Still, he felt a measure of pride that he'd managed it on his own.

When Grimes stopped outside an open bedroom door, Rudy paused beside him. "Bathroom first, please," he stated, feeling his bladder twinge. "And a toothbrush?"

If there was even a chance of getting a goodnight kiss from his mate, he wanted a fresh mouth for it.

Grimes nodded. "Of course." He pointed at the open door across the hall and told Gary, "If you want a separate room, that one's yours."

Gary nodded, taking a step toward it.

Then Grimes beckoned. "Bathroom is this way. Sorry, none of the rooms have an ensuite in this old Victorian."

"That's fine."

As far as Rudy was concerned, the luxury of an ensuite was a fairly recent development for the average homeowner. Of course, being one hundred sixty-two years old, he considered many things recent developments. He sure appreciated indoor plumbing, but he'd been much happier to go into electrical.

After accepting the toothbrush and boxer shorts from Chip, Rudy headed into the bathroom to take care of business. He looked longingly at the shower, but he didn't think he had the energy for it. Instead, Rudy used a soapy cloth to swiftly wash himself.

Once done, Rudy pulled on the boxer shorts and exited the room. He returned to the bedroom Grimes had indicated. Pausing in the doorway, he sucked in a surprised and appreciative breath. Rudy's mate stood beside the bed, and while he looked uncertain, he was holding a tube of something or other.

Gary turned away from the window he'd been staring out of and offered an uncertain smile. Holding up the ointment, he murmured, "I, uh, I hope you don't mind me being here. Um, just letting myself in."

Rudy stepped into the room, closing the door behind him. Turning back to face his mate, he admitted, "I will always want you here, Gary." Seeing the way his mate glanced around furtively, he knew he couldn't rush the man. "Okay, then," he continued, moving toward the opposite side of the bed as to where Gary stood. "I'm going to lie on the bed, and you do whatever you wish to me."

Excitement flooded Rudy as he pushed down the light blanket and sheet. As he eased onto the bed, he tried to keep his breathing steady as he thought about how, in the next moment or so, his mate would be joining him.

CHAPTER SIX

Gary eased toward the bed, unable to help the arousal that simmered through him. The prospect of getting his hands on all the gorgeous, tanned flesh on display before him was just too alluring. It had been a long time since he'd been intimate with anything other than his right hand.

And that's not changing now. This is just a massage.

Even his mental chastisement didn't do anything to ease the waves of desire buffeting his system. His dick was already hard behind the fly of his nice jeans, and he hadn't even touched the man, yet.

Stopping next to the bed, Gary tried to decide the best place to start.

"They told you a shifter has enhanced senses, like smell," Rudy murmured softly, turning his head to peer at him. "That means I can smell your arousal, my mate."

"Oh." Embarrassment surged through Gary, and he swallowed hard before whispering, "Sorry."

"I don't say that to embarrass you, Gary," Rudy countered.

"Then why?" Gary had to ask.

Rudy smiled at him, the expression somewhat lethargic. "I'm hard, too," he admitted. "Your scent, your presence, does that to me." He tipped his chin a bit, and he eyed Gary's body. "I just mean, you can't be comfortable like that. Plus, the oil could get on your clothes once you're kneeling beside me on the bed." Rudy's eyes narrowed a little, and he licked his lips. "No pressure, my mate, but perhaps you'd be more comfortable if you took off those jeans and that nice shirt."

Acting on instinct, Gary crossed his arms over his belly. He looked away and nibbled his bottom lip. Gary knew he didn't have a gorgeous body like Rudy.

Would his belly turn the man off? It had happened before.

His nerves caused his erection to begin to soften.

"Oh, my mate," Rudy crooned. Reaching out, he gripped Gary's wrist in a loose hold. "I don't know what just popped into your head, but it couldn't have been good." After another light squeeze, Rudy released him, saying, "I'm sorry, Gary. I didn't mean to pressure you."

Gary shook his head, realizing Rudy had gotten the wrong impression. "Not that," he whispered, sliding his hands up to rub at his opposite arms. "What if, um"—he paused a second, then forced himself to finish—"what if you don't like how I look?"

Rudy's brows shot up, a look of confusion creasing his features. "Not like the way you look?" Shaking his head just a smidge as he swept his gaze over Gary's frame, he immediately added, "That's not possible. You're perfect."

Scoffing, Gary rolled his eyes. "No, I'm fat."

"Not fat," Rudy countered, a growl entering his voice. "Sturdy, and I happen to like that."

Gaping, Gary stared at the man on the bed. "Y-You do?"

"Hell, yeah," Rudy replied emphatically. "I'm a shifter, with increased strength and speed. You being sturdy means I'm less likely to hurt you with my undeniable need for your delectable body."

Gary cocked his head, not having thought of it that way before. "Um, okay."

Still, Gary couldn't help but blush as he gripped the hem of his shirt. After a couple seconds of hesitation, he pulled his polo shirt over his head, leaving him in his white undershirt that clung way too much to his rounded belly. Gary couldn't force himself to meet Rudy's gaze and quickly turned to fold the fabric and place it on the dresser. Then he undid his fly and bent, shoving his jeans down and off, taking his shoes and socks with it.

The sound of Rudy sucking in a harsh breath, followed by a soft groan, caused Gary to peer over his shoulder at the man. He'd opened his mouth to ask what was wrong, but the appreciative, hungry look on Rudy's face told the tale.

"Oh," Gary whispered, surprise filling him.

Rudy snapped his focus to Gary's face, but the heat in his eyes remained. "You have a gorgeous ass, Gary," he stated, a soft growl filling his tone. "I look forward to the time when you'll allow me to squeeze it. Perfect handfuls."

Gary had always believed his ass to be too plump. Sitting at a desk for too many hours of the day could do that to a man. Plus, he loved food, and he hated working out.

"Y-You really like it?" Gary whispered, trying to peer over his shoulder, as if his ass had suddenly changed since the last time he'd looked at it.

Rudy's expression softened. "Yes, Gary. I really, *really* like it." Pushing up on one elbow, he half-rolled. He waved at his groin, openly showcasing the heavily tented fabric of the boxers. "See?"

"Oh." Gary didn't know what else to say.

Smiling, Rudy eased back onto his stomach. "Now that you're more comfortable, how about that massage?"

Relief filled Gary at the change in subject.

I can do this.

Picking up the tube of unscented massage oil that Payson had given to him, Gary returned to the side of the bed. He felt his cheeks warm, as he was ever mindful of Rudy staring at him with an expression of relaxed desire. It caused his belly to flutter, as if butterflies bounced within him, and his prick once again swelled.

As Gary climbed onto the bed near Rudy's feet, he suddenly appreciated that he wore boxer-briefs. While it didn't hide the fact that he was aroused, at least it wasn't quite so blatant as the boxers Rudy was wearing. As Gary poured the oil onto his left palm, it occurred to him that Rudy didn't seem to mind sharing that he was aroused by him.

Huh.

"You okay?"

Rudy's question yanked Gary out of his head, and he realized he must have been sitting there a moment or so . . . long enough for the other man to worry.

"Yeah, yeah," Gary quickly replied, closing the cap and setting the tube aside. "Just, um"—he thought quickly as he rubbed his palms together to warm the oil—"guess I'm on information overload, and I keep getting stuck in my head." Forcing a smile and hoping it didn't appear a bit dazed, Gary met Rudy's gaze and did his best to assure him. "I'll be okay."

"If there's anything I can do," Rudy began softly, his tone gentle.

Gary nodded, but he didn't reply. Instead, he lowered his hands to Rudy's calf and began to massage. He found plenty of tight muscle beneath his fingers and focused on something he could control . . . helping the man relax and recover from his ordeal.

"Oh, gods, Gary," Rudy murmured before letting out a deep sigh. "Your hands." He groaned softly. "Magick."

Smiling, Gary felt his cheeks heat anew. He bit his lower lip, uncertain what to say. Gary chose, "I'm glad I remember how to do this."

Rudy grunted, his toes twitching.

For a while, the only thing heard in the room were Rudy's soft grunts and groans mixed with the slap and slide of Gary's hands on the other man's flesh.

Gary moved from one limb to the next. Once he finished both legs, stopping midway up his thighs, because he didn't have the courage to go farther, he moved up the bed and focused on Rudy's arms. Then Gary moved to Rudy's neck and shoulders, starting to work down his back.

"Oh, gods," Rudy muttered, breaking the silence. "I'm so hard it hurts, baby."

Gary froze, his thumbs pausing where he'd been massaging down Rudy's spine. As he'd massaged him, he'd been doing his best to ignore his own throbbing erection. The chance to touch the sexy man had just been too titillating, and he couldn't stop the way his body responded, no matter how much he tried to keep his movements clinical.

"Shit." Rudy huffed a breath, moving his arms up the bed. "I shouldn't have said that." He groaned before mumbling, "Sorry. Your touch has melted my brain, and it just slipped out." Turning his head further, Rudy peered at him with one deeply dilated hazel eye. "I said I don't expect a happy ending, and that's still true. I guess . . . this is me warning you, if you don't want to get me off, you'd better stop now."

Gaping, Gary whispered, "I could get you off just from massaging your back? Without even touching you?"

"Yeah, baby," Rudy confirmed. "You so could." With a rueful smile, he admitted, "My balls are so full right now, heavy and aching, and my cock throbs. A couple ruts, and I'd be a goner."

Listening to Rudy's words, Gary felt his dick twitch, and he knew he was right there with him.

Could I? Am I brazen enough?

Rudy grimaced, then whispered, "I'm sorry, my mate. I'm sorry I can't control myself. Been so long." His voice darkened, and he sounded almost tortured. "And you're my mate, and you're touching me, helping me. This isn't how I should repay you. I—"

"I'm in the same boat," Gary blurted, stopping Rudy's self-flagellated ramblings. Before Rudy could say anything, he quickly added, "My dick hurts so badly. Touching you . . . I . . . can't even describe my response. I just—" Gary paused, uncertain how to explain or ask for what he desperately wanted.

After a few seconds of hesitation, Rudy whispered, "Can I touch you?"

"Yes," Gary cried, wanting that more than anything.

Slowly, carefully, as if worried Gary might change his mind, Rudy rolled onto his back.

Gary's attention was immediately snagged by the massive wet spot on Rudy's underwear, showcasing his flared crown behind the fabric.

"Come here, my mate," Rudy crooned, lifting his arms and gripping Gary's upper arms in a loose hold, even as he tugged gently. "Straddle me, baby."

Obeying, Gary eased his leg over Rudy's waist. He settled his weight on his soon-to-be lover's groin. The pressure on his balls felt exquisite, and Gary moaned softly as his breathing sped up.

"Yeah," Rudy murmured gruffly. "That's the way."

Rudy lowered one hand to Gary's hip while sliding the other around his upper back. He encouraged his body to lean over Rudy's, and he rested his still-slicked hands on the bigger man's shoulders. Gary rested his body along Rudy's own, suddenly wishing he'd had the courage to remove his shirt.

"Move with me, baby," Rudy encouraged, rocking his hips a little as he tugged on Gary's hip.

Gary couldn't have stopped himself if he'd tried. The pressure, the driving need for friction, burned through him. His blood fired through his veins as he began to move, rutting against the other man. Gary thought about reaching between them to lower their underwear, but the idea of giving up the pressure on his cock and balls, even for an instant, seemed too much to ask.

"Oh, god," Gary whined, feeling his balls tighten. The telltale tingle at the base of his spine told him he was seconds away from release. "Rudy."

"Yesss, Gary," Rudy hissed into his ear. "Do it," he urged, rocking under him. "Soak us with your seed. I want to feel it. Smell it." Rudy nipped at Gary's neck lightly before rumbling, "Then I'm gonna add to it. Make you smell like me."

Gary groaned as his orgasm burst through him. His balls pulled even tighter, and his cock pulsed, pouring spurt after spurt of seed into his underwear. He shook as heat and ecstasy fired through him, making him flush hot with the intensity.

While Gary wasn't certain how long he floated, when he came to, he lay on his side, facing Rudy. He felt the other man easing his underwear from him. Gary would have felt embarrassed, except the other man was already nude.

"Just relax, my mate," Rudy murmured, rubbing a palm over his hip. "You took care of me. Now let me take care of you." He touched the damp hem of Gary's shirt. "Let me take this off you."

Obediently, Gary lifted his arms even as he nodded.

Rudy smiled, clearly pleased, and he quickly eased Gary's shirt from him. Instead of tossing it off the side of the bed, as he'd done with the underwear, he used a clean side to wipe over first Gary's groin, then his own. After that, Rudy dropped it off the bed.

Finally, Rudy grabbed the blanket and top sheet and pulled them over them both. He wrapped his arms around Gary, cuddling him against his lean torso.

"I know it's presumptuous of me," Rudy murmured into Gary's hair. Then he cupped his jaw and gently urged him to meet his gaze. "May I have a goodnight kiss, then cuddle you for a little while?"

Gary hadn't lain with a lover after sex in . . . so very long, and he hadn't realized how much he'd missed it.

"Yes, please," Gary agreed, even though he knew it would just get him in deeper with the shifter who wanted him for all time.

When Rudy gently sealed his lips over Gary's and shared their first kiss, Gary decided he might not mind that so much, either.

CHAPTER SEVEN

Waking with his mate still in his arms, Rudy had never felt so blessed. He remained still, listening to Gary's even breathing. Staring at his young human, he reveled in the novelty of a quiet morning with his one and only in his arms.

Rudy had truly never thought it would happen to him. He'd thought he would end up dying in a cage. Instead, the lust for power exhibited by a couple of circles of witches drew the attention of the Four Horsemen of the Apocalypse, and Rudy was saved.

Go figure.

"Are you staring at me?"

Blinking, Rudy refocused on his mate and smiled at him. "Perhaps." He brushed a kiss to Gary's temple. "Good morning, my mate."

Gary's long black lashes lifted to reveal his morning-sleepy green eyes. "Morning," he whispered back, sounding shy. Then he squinted at him. "Um, I forgot to ask what you did with my glasses."

"They're right here on the nightstand." Rudy jerked his chin toward his left, indicating location, before fixing his gaze right back on Gary. "I hope you don't mind me taking the liberty of holding you all night."

A pink hue crept up Gary's neck and into his cheeks. "I liked it," he admitted. Then he swallowed hard and stated, "But now I really gotta get up because I need to pee."

Chuckling softly, Rudy eased his grip. "Me, too." Indicating the door, he offered, "You first."

"Thanks." Gary eased from the bed, his blush intensifying as he grabbed his jeans from the floor. "Um, never gone commando before," he muttered as he yanked the fabric up his legs. "It's weird."

Rudy levered up the bed, putting his back against the headboard. "Most shifters go commando on a regular basis," he revealed, pleased to have the strength back in his arms.

"Really?" Gary pulled on his polo shirt before turning to him. "Why?"

"Shifting in clothes can be hard on them," Rudy revealed with a shrug. "If I tried turning into my camel without getting naked first, whatever I was wearing would end up as ruined scraps."

"Oh." Gary nodded. "That makes sense." He shifted from foot to foot for a second, then asked, "Are you going to be okay? Do you need help?"

Pleasure filled Rudy upon learning that Gary worried for him. "I'm feeling so much better this morning," he assured. "I think after you're done, I'll shower and ask someone for clothes."

Gary nodded, then hurried to the door. When he opened it, he paused and bent. When he turned back, he was carrying a bundle of clothing.

"Guess someone thought of that." Gary returned to the bed and placed them on the blanket. "Um, see you downstairs?"

Realizing with a bit of disappointment that Gary needed a little space, Rudy nodded. "See you downstairs."

Rudy waited until Gary closed the bedroom door, then rose to his feet. After a few stretches, he realized he felt almost one hundred percent. He doubted he could run any marathons any time soon, but for the most part, the strength in his limbs had returned.

Thank the gods for that.

Checking out the articles of clothing, Rudy found a pair of sweats, a shirt, socks, and even a pair of tennis shoes that were his size. He decided someone had to have a good eye. After a quick look around the room, he didn't find any other clothes he could wear, and he didn't want to put the clean clothes on his oil-covered body.

Deciding the sheets would have to be cleaned anyway, Rudy stripped them from the bed and wrapped one around his body—toga style. He opened his bedroom door and peered down the hall. The door to the bathroom was already open, telling him that Gary had hurried.

With a sigh, Rudy headed inside the room.

Fifteen minutes later, feeling clean and refreshed, Rudy headed downstairs. He carried the dirty laundry. He spotted Chip and called the man's name.

"Where's the washing machine?" Rudy asked, lifting the indicated items. "Or is there a system you all use or a list to get on?"

Rudy figured, with so many men residing in one house, someone had to have organized something so everyone wasn't fighting for the washing machine.

"Oh, I'll take them," Chip told him, reaching for the sheets.

"Uh, well, there's underwear and a shirt in there, too." Rudy lowered his voice, hoping not too many people would overhear, since he didn't want to embarrass his lover. "That massage was something else."

Chip grinned. "Massages between mates have a way of getting out of hand fast," he commented back, his voice just as quiet. "It's okay. We're not shy here. We all handle each other's undergarments all the time, and if Gary's going to stay, then he'll get used to it." Cocking his head, Chip asked bluntly, "Is Gary going to stay?"

"I hope so," Rudy replied, handing over the bundle of cloth. Rubbing the back of his neck, he admitted, "At least until we know it's safe. If he wants to go home to Tennessee, I'll need to look into herds and shit in that area." With a shake of his head, Rudy admitted, "I didn't mind being a lone shifter when it was just me, but I need to make certain my mate is safe."

Nodding, Chip replied, "I totally understand." He lifted the laundry and stated, "I'll take care of this. Gary is in the dining room with a few others."

"Thanks."

After Chip headed away, Rudy went in search of the dining room. Fortunately, it was easy to find. He paused in the doorway and took in the occupants.

Gary sat beside Evan. Shannon was on Evan's other side. From the scent of things, a couple of the other guys there were bear shifters, too, but Rudy hadn't officially met them, yet.

Rudy really didn't like the fact that one of the men sat beside Gary, leaning close and engaging him in conversation. While he never wanted Gary to think he couldn't converse with friends, the way the other single shifter was eyeing his mate set his teeth on edge. His camel grumbled in his mind, and he barely managed to hold in his jealous snarl.

Shannon spotted Rudy, and he glanced from him to Gary, the bear, and back again. Shaking his head just a smidge, he turned back to the other bear. He threw a bit of toast at the guy, getting his attention.

"Hey, Val," Shannon rumbled. He pointed toward Rudy, so he began to approach. "Gary's mate is here. Can you move down a chair?"

"Gary's mate?" The bear shifter—Val, evidently—turned and peered at Rudy. His shoulders slumped as he heaved a sigh. As Val moved down a chair, dragging his plate and mug with him, he grumbled, "Of course the little cutie would be taken already."

"Yes, my cutie most certainly is." Rudy tipped his chin up

in silent thanks to Shannon, who smirked and ever-so-dis-creetly nodded. Then Rudy settled in Val's vacated chair and focused on Gary. "May I have a good morning kiss, my mate?"

Gary's cheeks pinked, but he whispered, "O-Okay."

Rudy would happily take it. He gently cradled Gary's jaw and leaned toward his mate. Lightly pecking his lips to his human's once, twice, before rubbing their lips together in a sensual glide.

While releasing Gary was difficult, Rudy did it. He relaxed back in his chair and glanced at the plates before the others. There were generous helpings of scrambled eggs with pep-pers and onions as well as some kind of hashbrown casserole. Bacon and sausage links appeared to round out the meal, and Rudy's stomach growled loudly in appreciation.

"Looks like someone worked up an appetite this morning," Shannon teased with a wink.

Shaking his head, spotting Gary's quickly flushing cheeks out of the corner of his eye, Rudy commented, "A gentleman does not discuss such things."

"I'll just get the deets later from Gary," Evan stated with a scoff. "Besties tell each other everything."

Smiling warmly at Gary, Rudy told his human, "That's completely up to you." Before his mate needed to answer, he rose and asked, "Do you want more of anything, Gary? I can bring it with my own plate of food."

"Um, just more coffee, please," Gary replied softly.

Rudy nodded, and just because he could, he bent and pecked a quick kiss to Gary's lips before heading into the kitchen. He smirked when he overheard Evan's whiney com-ment.

"You're just getting more coffee because I can't have any, yet."

Over the course of the next few days, Rudy did his best to be patient. He relished every chance he could to kiss Gary, doing it each time they passed in the halls. Keeping to his promise, Rudy spent most of his time checking the aging home's electrical. Gary was often busy working on one of the guy's laptops or spending time with Evan, helping the man learn how to become a warlock and control his magick. Occasionally, they played video games. On rare occasions, Gary would come help Rudy, holding wire or tools.

Rudy loved those times the most.

Evan had warned Rudy not to rush Gary. Evidently, the man had a heightened flight response. He'd had a number of exes complain about his weight, his inactivity sitting behind a computer, and to such ridiculous things as his choice of clothing and haircut. Rudy thought Gary was perfect just the way he was, and he took every opportunity to tell his mate that.

"Hey, how's it going?"

Rudy lifted his attention from the electrical outlet he was rewiring and saw Olson standing in the room that would probably be used as an office. "Good." Peering up from where he sat on the floor, he shrugged. "Just tedious. I should be able to let you turn the power back on in about half an hour." Pointing, Rudy indicated the outlets on the other wall. "Just two more after this one."

Olson nodded, then lowered to one knee and settled beside him. "I'm not worried about that." He lowered his voice. "Look, I know I'm new to the shifter way of life, but . . ." Pausing, Olson rubbed the back of his neck before refocusing on him. "And I don't mean to overstep, but do you think it's such a good idea to be spending so much time on my house instead of on wooing your mate?"

Blowing out a quiet breath, Rudy grimaced. "You're not overstepping," he murmured, putting down his tools. "And

I'm honestly not sure." Rudy grimaced as he admitted, "I've never had to woo anyone before, and Evan told me to give Gary a little space and time to come to terms with what we are to each other. I'm a little confused on how to do both."

Rubbing his jaw, Olson scowled at nothing. His expression appeared a little vacant. "Well," he started slowly. "I overheard Gary saying something to Yuma. He was asking if a shifter could be wrong about their mate because you've never talked to him about wanting to bond."

"Shit," Rudy muttered, shaking his head. "I know I was half asleep on the sofa when the guys explained bonding to Gary, so he knows what it entails. I haven't wanted to push him, but I guess I pushed him the opposite way with my silence." Sighing, Rudy scrubbed his fingers through his shaggy hair. "I'm shit at this, aren't I?"

Olson chuckled softly. "Fortunately, in a house full of busybodies, it's never too late to get help to fix it." Cocking his head, he eyed him. "I have an idea, and it just may help him connect with your animal, too."

Rudy listened as Olson spoke, liking the plan more and more.

CHAPTER EIGHT

"What's up?" Gary asked, lifting his attention from the laptop where he was working. Lamar had been kind enough to loan him one of the gang's, so Gary could get into his cloud storage and complete some projects. When he'd come to Louisiana, he hadn't intended to stay for an impromptu vacation, and he still had deadlines for a few clients to meet.

"Can you save that and come with me?" Evan asked, eyeing him with his hands on his hips. "I want to show you something."

Gary nodded. "Give me two minutes."

He figured Evan had learned some new spell from Draven or Tim, and he wanted to show it off. Gary didn't mind. After all, he found Evan's new and burgeoning talents fascinating. While he would never admit it to anyone, he was even a little jealous.

After finishing a mathematical equation on the spreadsheet, Gary saved his work, uploaded it to his cloud storage account, and logged off the system. Then he shut down the computer and closed the lid. Standing slowly, he swept his gaze over Evan's leg. His friend wore shorts, and there was just a little swelling left beneath the bandage.

"How's the leg?" Gary couldn't help but ask as Evan wrapped his arm around Gary's and started them walking. "Feeling okay?" His bestie had been enjoying coffee again for the last couple of days, and he'd even joined him in a glass of wine the evening before, so Gary figured he had to be doing well for Eli to give him the okay.

Evan nodded eagerly. "Just fine. Almost all healed." With a wink, he added, "Gotta love swifter healing after being claimed. So very nice."

"Uh-huh," Gary replied non-committedly. He hadn't told Evan that he and Rudy hadn't discussed bonding . . . like . . . ever. He didn't know how to bring it up to his lover. Gary thought maybe the shifter should have been pushing for it, right?

So why isn't he?

When they bypassed the stairs, Gary asked, "Where are we going?"

"Outside," Evan replied. "Have you been outside since you arrived?"

"Uh, no," Gary admitted. Unable to help himself, he added dryly, "I'm not much of an outdoorsy guy, remember?"

Evan chuckled. "I know, but you'll love this. I promise." Then his brows furrowed, and he muttered, "Well, I hope you will. I think it'd be cool."

Confused, Gary asked, "What are you talking about?"

"You'll see," Evan answered evasively. "It's just out front."

As they approached the front door, it was opened from the outside, and Chip appeared. He grinned widely at them. "Oh, there you are." He glanced over his shoulder, then faced them again. "I was just about to come looking." Opening the door wider, Chip added, "Everything's ready."

"Ready?" Gary glanced between his best friend and the sweet shifter who was becoming a good friend. "Ready for what?"

Chip's tanned complexion actually darkened a smidge, betraying that he blushed. "Um, your surprise," he murmured, backing away and throwing up an arm. "Ta-da! Your very own camel ride."

Gary stepped onto the porch and stopped, gaping at the sight ten feet in front of the porch. A camel he'd seen only once before knelt on the ground. There was a pair of thick ropes holding a blanket onto the hump with a handle near the front.

Upon seeing Gary, the camel rumbled, the noise sounding suspiciously like a greeting.

"Oh wow." Gary found himself riveted to the spot, staring in surprise. "Is that, um?"

"Yep," Evan confirmed. "That's your shifter in his animal form." He tugged at Gary's arm, forcing him to take a couple of steps. "We noticed you hadn't had a chance to bond with him, yet, so . . . go take a ride."

"I-I'm supposed to r-ride a c-camel?" Gary murmured in disbelief, dragging his feet. "I've never even ridden a horse."

Grimes stood near the camel's head and moved toward them. "Of course not," he stated, his deep voice rumbling a bit. "You're not riding *a* camel. You're riding *your* camel. Your *mate's* camel. Remember, just because he's in camel form, he still knows exactly who you are, and what you mean to him."

"O-Oh . . . right," Gary whispered. "Forgot about that."

By then, Evan had urged Gary forward enough that he stood near the camel's — *uh, Rudy's* — side. After swallowing hard, Gary murmured, "Um, hi, Rudy."

Rudy's camel rumbled a greeting as his head turned on its long neck. The beast ever-so-gently rubbed its cheek against Gary's chest and belly. As it did so, the camel made some sort of contented burbling sound.

"Okay." Grimes stepped close. "Here's how you mount." He pointed at a loop of rope fastened near the bottom of the blanket. "We don't have a traditional saddle, so we improvised a little, but I'm pretty sure we got your leg length right. If not, I'll adjust it. Put your foot there, Gary."

Hesitating, Gary peered at the large beast before him. Then he glanced at the others, seeing their expectant expressions. His heart pounded a bit wildly, and as much as he wished he could refuse, he didn't want to hurt their feelings, either.

Focusing on the camel, Gary took in the warm amber gaze of the kneeling beast. He realized he'd seen that same look so many times in Rudy's eyes. He finally understood what they meant about the shifter being cognizant in their animal form. The camel waited expectantly, wanting to share time with Gary.

Gary took a deep, fortifying breath, then lifted his foot to the rope stirrup. He reached up and gripped the handle in front of the top of the hump. After a couple of bounces on his foot to get a rhythm going, Gary jumped and swung his leg over.

With a squeak, Gary felt himself begin to slide off the other side. The camel whipped his head to the right and pressed his head against Gary's side, holding him in place. Getting his balance, Gary found the other stirrup. He even found a sort of padded seat situated at the backside of the camel's hump, offering him support so he didn't slide backward.

Once Gary felt sort of stable, he smiled at the camel and murmured, "Thanks, Rudy."

Rudy burbled again as he rubbed his head against Gary's leg. Then the beast straightened his neck before shifting its weight.

"Now remember," Grimes called. "He'll get his back legs under him first, so hang on tight and try to lean back a little. Ready?"

Gary didn't think so, but he nodded anyway.

Grimes stood on one side while Chip and Evan were on his other side.

Then . . . Rudy began to rise.

Clamping his lips together, Gary managed to hold in his *eep* of surprise. He clung to the rope as tightly as possible as Rudy rocked forward, then back, rising to his feet. By the time Rudy was standing, Gary's fingers hurt from gripping so hard.

"You all right up there, Gary?" Grimes called. "Comfortable?"

Gary forced himself to look down . . . and thought the ground was so much farther away than it should be. "Um, I-I think I'm okay."

"I read online that you should try to keep your muscles loose," Chip advised, smiling up at him. "You'll want to sway with the camel's movements. Okay?"

"Uh, sure."

What else am I supposed to say?

"Rudy is going to make a couple of laps around the yard while you get used to it," Grimes explained. "And we'll walk beside you. Let us know if you're experiencing any problems, and we'll see what we can do to adjust your seat."

Gary nodded, and Rudy started walking.

At first, the camel's ambling gait felt awkward and uncomfortable. He felt certain he was going to be thrown off any second. By the second lap, Gary started to understand the movements, and he followed Chip's advice, swaying slightly.

"There ya go," Grimes encouraged. "You look like you're getting it."

"Um, yeah." Gary felt pleasure of a different kind infuse him. "Yeah, I guess I am."

Once Gary allowed himself to relax, he thought it was pretty cool.

"Okay, guys," Grimes stopped at the porch and waved. "Have a nice walk."

"Walk?" Gary squeaked. "Walk where?"

Grimes just laughed and waved again.

Chip shook his head and elbowed his big mate in the stomach. "If you run into any problems, you can just give a shout for help." He pointed toward the woods. "There are plenty of guys out running, and they'll swing by to give you a hand."

"Okay." Gary still wasn't certain how he felt about going

on an actual walk.

"And I want a ride on Rudy's camel when you get back," Evan hollered, grinning broadly.

For some reason, Gary found himself scowling, and he turned away from Evan without answering. He couldn't explain it, but it dawned on him swiftly. Gary didn't want to share riding his lover with anyone.

And not like that.

"Aww, you can ride my bear, babe."

Recognizing Shannon's voice, Gary hoped the man would distract Evan when they returned. That way he wouldn't be tempted to bitch-slap his bestie.

Geez, since when am I possessive like this?

Except, with Rudy, Gary definitely was.

Rudy eased between trees, following a path only he seemed to know. Gary thought about trying to talk to him, but he didn't want to frustrate the shifter. After all, it wasn't as if he had vocal cords for him to speak back.

In the end, Gary did make a few random comments. Things that he wouldn't require a response to. He thanked Rudy for taking him for a ride and showing him the forest. Gary made comments about how he sat behind a desk too much, and how he would really enjoy getting out more with Rudy.

Rumbling softly, Rudy made pleased-sounding grunts.

Gary smiled and fell silent.

They rode for a few more minutes, Rudy always weaving between trees in a way that left Gary with plenty of clearance. Finally, a small clearing opened up before them. To Gary's surprise, a blanket had been spread out in it, and a couple of baskets rested upon it.

Rudy reached the edge of the blanket and stopped. Turning his head, he rumbled softly.

An instant later, Gary realized it had been a warning. The camel bent its front legs and slowly started to kneel. He clutched the ropes tightly, clinging to the shifter's harness.

Once Rudy knelt on the ground, he turned his head and made an encouraging burbling noise.

"Oh, right." Gary realized it was time to get off. "Um, just a second."

After a moment, Gary figured out the logistics of dismounting. Still, with an ungraceful flop, he lost his balance and ended up sprawled on the blanket. Rudy's camel nuzzled him with his head, rumbling questioningly.

Gary chuckled as he sat up. Rubbing the camel's head, he reveled in the odd freedom being able to pet the beast gave him. The animal seemed to enjoy it, too, for he grumbled some more and rubbed against him.

After a couple of minutes, the camel drew away.

Then the popping and snapping noises of a shifter changing forms filled the clearing.

Fighting back a wince, Gary felt relief that Rudy didn't scream in pain that time. Over the past few days, he'd seen other shifters change back and forth. They weren't shy about it, stripping and shifting or vice-versa. Most of them were pretty quick about it, altering forms within half a minute or less.

Rudy wasn't quite that fast, but before long, Gary's naked lover crouched on the ground before him. Instead of rising, he moved to his hands and knees and crawled onto the blanket beside him, easing away from the ropes and blanket that had been on him.

"Hi," Rudy murmured, continuing toward him until he levered over him. "Thank you for coming."

Before Gary could come up with a response, Rudy captured his mouth, pushing his tongue between his lips.

Gary gripped Rudy's shoulders and clung, only too happy to relax on the blanket with his shifter.

Chapter Nine

Rudy knew he needed words. He needed to talk to Gary, but with his mate pliable beneath him, he found it difficult to remember why. With his human kissing him back, arching into him, Rudy never wanted the moment to end.

The feel of fabric scraping against his skin reminded Rudy that while he was nude, Gary was not. He knew it was an easy thing to fix . . . if he could stop kissing the man. Rudy just loved the taste of his human so very much.

Finally, mostly because his lungs were screaming for air, Rudy broke the kiss. He panted harshly as he stared down at the man he was quickly falling in love with. Rudy couldn't imagine a moment, let alone a day, where he couldn't have this human by his side.

"I want to claim you." Rudy would forever blame his tactless words on a mix of having all his blood in his dick coupled with a lack of oxygen. "Gods, I didn't mean to blurt it out like that."

"You do?"

Gary sounded so damn surprised, and it nearly broke Rudy's heart.

"I know we haven't talked about it," Rudy began, doing his best to ignore the ache in his shaft. "But I didn't want to pressure you." Grimacing, he shook his head while keeping his gaze pinned on Gary. "But that's no excuse for not at least discussing it."

Sliding his fingers through Gary's hair, Rudy massaged his mate's scalp as he rested his weight on that elbow. "Yes,

Gary," he stated, his voice still a bit rough from kissing. "I want to claim you. I want to slide my hard shaft into your body, and give you as much pleasure as possible." Skimming his free palm down Gary's side, he began teasing up under his shirt. "I want to make you orgasm over and over, until you pass out from the pleasure of it as I sink my canines into your flesh and drink your blood, bonding our life strands for all eternity." After a few heartbeats, where Gary just stared at him with wide green eyes, his be-speckled expression one of clear surprise, Rudy added, "Then I want to spend the rest of my life figuring out how to keep pleasing you, over and over. I want to be yours as much as I want you to be mine. Can we do that?"

A second later, a wide smile curved Gary's lips. His green eyes darkened with lust. "Yeah, Rudy," he murmured softly. Then he admitted, "I was worried when you didn't say anything about it."

"I'm sorry I made you doubt, my mate," Rudy stated, mentally berating himself for his foolishness. "I've been alone for so long that I seem to have forgotten how to communicate."

Gary rubbed his palms over Rudy's back as he shrugged one shoulder. "I wasn't much better."

"We'll both work on it," Rudy stated decidedly before pecking a kiss to his lover's lips. Peering into his human's eyes, he asked, "May I undress you?"

To Rudy's surprise and disappointment, Gary shook his head.

"No?" Rudy lifted a little, trying to figure out his misunderstanding. "But—"

"I'll undress me," Gary claimed, his eyes twinkling with mischief. "I need you, and I don't want to wait." Then a wash of pink erupted on his neck. "I've been playing with myself in the shower every day, so I probably won't need a lot of prep, but do you have lube?"

Rudy moaned, a hard shudder rolling through him as he thought of his wet, soapy mate playing with his ass. "Next shower, we're taking it together," he vowed as he eased away from Gary. "And yeah. I know there's some lube in one of these baskets."

"Get it," Gary ordered, and Rudy was only too happy to obey.

Coming up empty in the first basket—it was full of food—Rudy began pulling everything out of the second—utensils, clothes, wet naps, and—"Got it!" Rudy cried triumphantly, yanking the tube from the bottom.

When Rudy turned around, he nearly swallowed his tongue. True to Gary's word, he'd stripped. He lay on his back in the middle of the blanket. His body was flushed, probably due to the two fingers he already had in his chute as well as the way he fondled his prick.

Any other time, Rudy would have loved to have sat and watched Gary pleasure himself. Except, right then, he needed something else even more. He needed to bond with his mate.

"Oh, Gary," Rudy moaned, crawling back to him. "You're so sensual. So gorgeous."

From the slight shadowing in Gary's eyes, Rudy would bet that his mate didn't believe him.

Someday he will.

With that vow in mind, Rudy popped the cap on the lube. He poured a liberal amount onto his throbbing shaft before gripping himself and jacking quickly, spreading it. Then he poured more lube onto his fingers, closed the cap, and dropped it onto the blanket.

With his free hand, Rudy gently gripped Gary's wrist. He pulled his lover's hand free of his chute, only to replace it with a lubed finger of his own. Rudy groaned softly upon feeling the heat of his human's body surround his digit, and he quickly added a second one.

As Rudy stretched and lubed his mate, he levered back

over him. He rested his weight on his forearm so he could capture Gary's lips in a slow, sensual kiss. All the while, Rudy opened his human as quickly as he dared.

Just as Gary had warned, in a fairly short amount of time, Rudy thought his mate was ready.

Gary turned his head, breaking the kiss, only to gasp, "Now, Rudy. Oh, god. Please now." He tipped his head and met Rudy's gaze. "I need you . . . my mate."

Groaning roughly, Rudy practically vibrated with need upon hearing those two little words. "My mate," he repeated as he eased his fingers free of Gary's body. "Yessss," he hissed, gripping the base of his dick and guiding it to Gary's prepared hole. "Yesss, I'm yours."

To Rudy's pleasure, Gary wrapped not only his arms around his shoulders, but his legs around his waist. He tipped his ass in invitation . . . an invitation Rudy would never be able to resist. With a hard rock of his hips, he popped the head of his erection past Gary's guardian muscle, sinking it into the sweetest heat he had ever experienced.

"Oh," Gary gasped, but his muscles remained loose, telling Rudy that his exclamation was one of pleasure.

Rudy groaned his own enjoyment as he began to ease forward, then back, then forward again. He sank deeper and deeper into his lover with each pass. Gripping Gary's ass cheek in one palm, Rudy hitched his hips up a little higher as he spread him wide.

Then Rudy drove forward, embedding himself balls deep inside his mate.

"Rudy!" Gary cried his name, his body arching and his chute muscles clamping onto Rudy in a vice-like grip.

"Here, my mate," Rudy muttered through clenched teeth. He rested his forehead against Gary's, peering into his eyes through the lenses of his glasses, reveling in their heavy-lidded look. "Right here."

Gary panted softly, and Rudy waited. His human's muscles contracted and released along his length in a delicious, ball-tingling enticement, but he remained steady. Rudy needed his mate relaxed, comfortable, and ready for what was to come.

Finally, after a moment where just dragging enough air into his lungs was a feat, Rudy felt Gary's body relax. "You with me, my mate?" Rudy murmured, lowering his head to nuzzle at Gary's temple. "You feeling okay?"

"Yeah," Gary replied thickly. "You feel so good." His voice was husky with arousal, and his fingernails dug into Rudy's shoulder blades. "Bigger than I expected. Need you to move."

Rudy grinned, not only at Gary's praise, but at his demand. "Anything for you, my mate," he promised as he began to move. "Anything at all."

After easing out most of the way, Rudy adjusted his angle just a little and thrust back into him. He heard Gary's moan, felt his shudder, and grinned against the sweaty flesh of his mate's neck, knowing he'd found it. Memorizing that spot, Rudy began long-dicking his human in smooth, swift ruts, nailing his prostate over and over.

Before long, with a cry of ecstasy, Gary called his name and came. His seed coated their skin, the scent perfuming the air. His chute muscles clamped onto Rudy's shaft, and he didn't bother fighting what he craved.

As Rudy's balls contracted, and he shot spurt after spurt of seed into Gary's willing body, he opened his mouth. He felt his canines lengthen, and he quickly wrapped them around the flesh where his mate's neck met his shoulder. After laving the area with his tongue once, twice, Rudy sank his teeth deep into Gary's flesh.

When the first rush of Gary's life-fluid flowed across his tongue, Rudy groaned. His taste buds sang, and his senses buzzed. He swallowed quickly and sucked for more, needing it more than air. Rudy imagined he could feel their life-threads joining, and he reveled in that knowledge.

Rudy felt Gary come apart in his arms once more, jerking and trembling through another orgasm. The squeeze to his prick combined with the exquisite flavor of his mate's blood produced sparks, which fired through Rudy, and he came again, pouring several more bursts of cum into his mate.

Dark spots danced across Rudy's vision, and he barely managed to catch his weight on his forearms before he landed ungainly on top of his lover. He panted roughly through his nose as he eased his teeth free. Rudy licked over the bite mark, sealing it, and leaving behind an impressive claiming scar.

Satisfaction thrumming through him, Rudy smiled smugly at the sight of it.

"Wow," Gary mumbled, his voice rough. "That was . . . amazing."

"Yes, it was," Rudy agreed, mouthing kisses up his neck and capturing Gary's mouth.

For several long moments, Rudy took his time exploring Gary's mouth anew. His senses languid and comfortable, he broke the kiss, took a breath, and dove back in. After several minutes of that, he finally rested his forehead back against Gary's and let out a contented sigh, enjoying the feel of his lover's hands stroking up and down his back.

He also enjoyed the feel of his cock still embedded in Gary's ass. Still mostly hard, his desire banked to a simmer, but not yet sated, he relished the connection.

Rudy felt Gary clench and release his channel a couple of times, and he groaned softly at the sweet sensations it caused in his gut.

"I-I know you came." Gary said the words, but he sounded uncertain.

"Mmm-hmmm." Rudy didn't want his lover worried about that. Lifting his head, he grinned at Gary. "Twice."

Gary's brows furrowed, almost disappearing behind the gold rims of his glasses. "But you're still hard."

Rudy shrugged one shoulder negligently. "You do that to me, Gary," he replied simply. "But my shoulders are getting sore, so let's find a more comfortable position."

Before Gary could question him, or protest, Rudy slid his arms under his mate's shoulders and his ass. Then he rolled them. Once Rudy landed on his back, he relaxed, rubbing up and down Gary's back. At the same time, he bent his knees and spread his legs, placing his feet flat. That caused Gary's legs to spread wider, allowing Rudy to keep his erection buried deep inside his mate.

Sighing, Rudy began teasing his fingertips over Gary's flesh, exploring once more. "I love the feel of your skin, so smooth and soft." He pecked a kiss to Gary's temple, then peered into his mate's eyes when his human rested his hand on his chest and his chin upon his hand. "So, are you hungry? Or can we stay just like this for a few minutes?"

To emphasize his point, Rudy rolled his hips, rutting in and out of Gary's body.

Gary moaned, and he knew he was nudging the man's prostate.

Perfect.

Rudy could imagine them in this position often, enjoying not just the afterglow, but also the simple connection that came from their bodies being joined.

"I can wait to eat," Gary told him, panting softly. "But separating is going to hurt if the cum dries."

"I'm willing to risk it if you are." Rudy teased his cock in and out of Gary once more.

Gary groaned and relaxed more heavily upon him. "Yeah," he murmured, arousal deepening his voice once more. "Yeah. Just like this."

Yep. Perfect.

Chapter Ten

After a half-hour of cuddling and talking softly together, Rudy rutted into Gary slowly, driving him out of his mind. He came again—twice, since Rudy once again bit him. As Gary came down off his cloud of endorphins, he felt Rudy ease his softening prick from his chute. Then his lover carefully settled him on the blanket, separating their bodies with a bit of uncomfortable tugging.

Gary groaned as the unfamiliar sensation of cum dribbling from him tickled his backside. As odd as it felt, he decided it was better than the stings from tugging dried semen. He adjusted his hips as he watched Rudy crawl to one of the baskets.

A moment later, Rudy returned with several wet nap packets.

When his lover opened one and reached toward him, his intent to clean him clear, Gary eased to a sitting position and took the item. "I know you want to care for me, but I'm not ready for that yet," he claimed. Seeing Rudy's questioning look, Gary recalled their first time together, and how his lover had cleaned him. With a roll of his eyes as he began to clean himself, Gary stated, "That first time, you'd totally rocked my world, and I was sort of half-asleep through it."

Rudy hummed as he opened another wet nap. "Hmmm." He smirked. "A challenge then. To make you half-asleep from pleasure, so I get the honor of cleaning you."

Gary barked a laugh and shook his head. "Only you would think that was a challenge."

With an eyebrow waggle, Rudy continued cleaning himself. Once he was finished, he began pulling out the food. He didn't even seem inclined to dress first, and when Gary grabbed his jeans, Rudy gripped his wrist.

"Must you?" Rudy asked softly. A warm smile curved the corners of his lover's lips as he swept his gaze over him. "I like looking at you. You're beautiful."

For a few seconds, Gary nibbled his bottom lip as he fought down a blush. He thought the man needed his eyes checked. Except, seeing Rudy's hopeful expression, he gave in and nodded.

The grin Rudy gave him banished the rest of Gary's discomfort.

For the next hour, they ate, drank, and cuddled together. They talked about their pasts as well as their desires for the future. Even though they'd been sleeping in the same bed each night, they hadn't done a whole lot of talking, having spent most of their days doing their own things.

Rudy ended up apologizing for that, too—twice—and Gary had assured him that it was both their mistakes, and they would work on it.

Gary discovered they wanted much the same thing out of life. They were both homebodies, who enjoyed quiet evenings and the company of good friends, seeing as neither spoke much to family anymore. Rudy even revealed that he'd thrown himself into Olson's electrical work because it kept him out of the thick of things with the gang. His work was relatively quiet.

Kinda like my private accounting business. Quiet and mostly solitary.

When Rudy expressed his concern about their safety if they returned to Tennessee, Gary admitted to wanting to stay near Evan, which meant the gang, since his buddy had a lot to learn . . . for years.

To Gary's relief, Rudy seemed pleased.

Making out led to another round of fucking, and by the time Rudy started explaining how to refasten the makeshift saddle-rigging to his camel's back, Gary was deliciously sore.

"Uh, I'm not certain I'll remember all that," Gary admitted, staring at the ropes.

"Okay, let's do it this way." Rudy quickly untied the second rope. He left the first one intact and stepped through the hoop, tucking it under his armpits. "As I shift, just make certain this rope stays in front of my growing hump. Can you do that?"

Gary nodded slowly. "Okay."

Rudy then pointed at the blanket lying over his back. "Then stretch this over my hump and tie the second line under my belly." Smiling crookedly, he told him, "It won't be perfect, but it'll be good enough to get us back to the house."

"Got it." At least, Gary hoped so.

After pecking one more kiss to Gary's lips, Rudy crouched and started to shift. His body swiftly expanded, and Gary found himself staring in amazement. The saddle started to slide down Rudy's back, and Gary jumped forward and adjusted the rope, making sure it ended up where his shifter had ordered.

Once Rudy had completed his shift, he stood quietly while Gary tugged, pulled, and adjusted everything into place . . . to the best of his ability, anyway. Then his camel knelt, and Gary climbed aboard. After Rudy had returned to his feet, Gary peered around the clearing.

"Oh, what about the stuff?"

Rudy brayed softly as he shook his head.

Gary assumed that meant someone else would worry about it. He figured someone else had set it up, after all. As Rudy started walking, Gary felt his cheeks heat, recalling Grimes's words—there were others running around in case he needed help with anything.

Ugh. I hope no one saw us.

Oh well. Too late now.

Clinging to the rope, Gary once again tried to find the camel's walking rhythm. He found it after a few minutes, and he started peering around, enjoying the ride back. Gary was thinking about how to ask to come out again when a large, black-maned lion bounded toward them from between cypress trees.

Tensing, Gary stared at it. Even knowing it had to be one of the shifters—Grimes, if he wasn't mistaken—he still felt a fissure of fear. After all, it was a frickin' lion!

Gary was just about to start relaxing when, instead of falling into step beside them, it nipped at Rudy's hocks. The camel grumbled, turning its head to focus on the cat. The lion growled, pinning its ears, then went for Rudy's hocks again.

"Do you need us to hurry?" Gary guessed.

Grimes nodded and chuffed, prancing in place as he glanced around the forest.

Feeling the hairs on his nape stand on end, Gary patted Rudy, saying, "Um, I guess you gotta speed up, Rudy."

Grumbling, Rudy gave him a look that was clearly one of concern.

"I'll hold tight," Gary promised, hoping he could do as he said.

After a huff of agitation, Rudy picked up his pace.

His shuffling became more pronounced, and Gary struggled to keep up with the sway. He tightened his grip, tensing, only to realize that jostled him even worse. Blowing out a breath, Gary did his best to relax again, so he could move with the odd motion.

Gary felt as if he was just starting to get it when the crack of gunfire echoed between the trees.

Rudy picked up the pace, increasing his speed once more.

Yelping in surprise, Gary clung as best he could. At least,

at that speed, it felt like more of a rocking motion. As long as he stayed loose, Gary realized he could ride without too much trouble.

Another crack of gunfire reached them just as the old Victorian appeared through the trees. There seemed to be organized chaos in the yard as Kontra hollered orders. The big man appeared livid as he led the way into the woods with Mutegi and Sam, the pack's Texas longhorn bull beta—all three in human form.

Coming to a stop in front of the house, Gary looked around and realized no other animal was in sight. Even Grimes hadn't joined them in the yard. Everyone else milling about was in human form.

"You okay, Gary?" Evan called, peering up at him. "Sorry, Rudy. You need to stay a camel for a few moments, just in case."

After burbling his understanding, Rudy slowly knelt.

Gary swiftly dismounted. While he had to flail his arms, at least he didn't fall on his ass again. Evan grabbed his arm, lending him support.

As soon as Gary caught his balance, he rushed to Rudy's head. He wrapped his arms around his camel shifter's neck and whispered in his ear, "Are you okay?" Petting the animal, he continued, "You didn't get shot, did you?"

Rudy didn't seem upset or injured. The camel rubbed against Gary's stomach, nuzzling, seeming to enjoy the attention.

Just as Gary turned to ask what was going on, Alpha Kontra appeared between the trees. He was pushing one stranger, while Sam ushered another. Mutegi glared at them both, looking imperious.

"Gods, what meatheads." Kontra's snarled words just reached Gary's ears. Then the alpha raised his voice and called, "Draven or Prudhoe? You around?"

"I'm here, Kontra." The deep-voiced Prudhoe—a bald-headed, heavily built man—rounded the side of the house. For just an instant, his blue eyes appeared to flash lavender. "How can I help?"

Kontra sighed deeply. "Mind alterations."

"Of course." Prudhoe's smile appeared predatory. "What seems to be the trouble?"

"These yahoos spotted a couple of our wolves while out gator hunting." Kontra growled as he shook the collar of the burly, older-looking guy he held and added, "And it ain't gator season."

"Ah, so they should respect hunting laws and forget they saw any wolves."

"Exactly," Kontra agreed. He glared at the smaller, more timid-looking man being held by Sam. "This one, too, and we need to know if they mentioned wolves to anyone."

"Of course," Prudhoe responded, stopping before them. Once more, his eyes turned lavender, and now, they appeared to glow. "Let's take a look and see what makes you tick, human."

When Prudhoe touched the struggling man's temple, he instantly stilled. Within seconds, Prudhoe had released him and turned toward the second one.

Unable to help himself, Gary asked, "Is he a vampire, too?"

"Uh-uh," Evan replied with a shake of his head. "Fae."

"Fae?" Gary hissed back. "That's a thing?"

"It's a thing." A man with a melodious tenor moved to stand next to Gary. He winked one of his lavender eyes. "There are a couple of us around. I'm Elron."

"Wow," Gary whispered, staring at the slender man. "Guess I still have a few things to learn."

"Indeed."

Just as Elron finished saying the word, the ground began to tremble. A loud bugle rent the air. Breaking cypress trees instead of going around them, a huge elephant barreled toward Kontra and those with him.

Everyone in the group stopped and stared, looking more confused and concerned than afraid — well, all except for the man Prudhoe had yet to touch.

Prudhoe pulled his hand away from the smaller, trembling man, his blond brows drawing together. "Alpha?"

Kontra shrugged. "Not sure." Lifting his voice to be heard over the thudding earth, he called, "What's wrong, elephant?"

The elephant skidded to a stop just in time so he didn't hit Sam. Wrapping his trunk around the gaping, pale-featured man in Sam's grip, the elephant tugged the guy away from the beta. The elephant backed up, holding the guy against him as he surveyed the group.

"Elephant, is he —" Kontra didn't get a chance to finish.

The elephant whirled with a surprising amount of agility, then began rushing away, taking the guy with him.

Elron chuckled softly. "Another one bites the dust."

"Oh, for the love of Pete," Kontra grumbled. Waving toward the retreating beast, he hollered, "Payson, Vane. Track him, but don't engage." As a hyena and a wolf appeared only to streak after the elephant, Kontra rubbed the back of his neck. "What is it with this swamp?" Then he turned his attention to Prudhoe. "Guess not that guy." He used his thumb to indicate the man Prudhoe had already touched. "Let's talk about this one." Except, then Kontra must have noticed Rudy waiting patiently. He lifted a hand and made a shooing motion. "You're good to shift."

Immediately, Rudy did just that. As soon as he could, he stood and swept Gary into his arms. "I'm so sorry I had to jostle you so," he rumbled, his tone full of remorse. "I had to follow the enforcer's urgings."

"It's okay. Really. Maybe sometime we can try that again

but without the fear of gunshots," Gary told him, rubbing Rudy's chest. As his shifter nodded in response, Gary noticed he was being carried into the house and upstairs. "I'm really fine. Nothing a hot bath on sore muscles won't cure."

"Then that's exactly what we'll do," Rudy declared. His expression turned beseeching as he added, "Our bond is new. I need to know you're well."

"Okay," Gary repeated, accepting Rudy's shifter nature.

Gary couldn't say he minded, either, not one bit. When Rudy carried him into the bathroom, turned on the tub water, and began stripping him, he knew his life had just become so much more interesting.

Interesting and better.

Following along happily, Gary allowed Rudy to help him into the bath. He sat in his lover's arms, enjoying the stroke of the other man's palms as he glided them over every inch of Gary's skin, and Gary reveled in his lover's sweet caresses and gentle ministrations.

No matter what changes I have to make, this man, right here, makes it all worth it.

ABOUT THE AUTHOR

Charlie started writing fantasy when she was eight, and after stumbling onto her first erotic romance at age nineteen, she realized her true calling. She now focuses on writing gay erotic romance, normally of the paranormal variety, with heroes of all kinds. With the help and support of her husband, Charlie finally fulfilled one of her life-long goals . . . move to acreage with her horses. You can often find her curled up with her laptop and a cup of tea or glass of wine, creating her next adventure. Charlie enjoys exploring the mountains of her new Oregon home on horseback, 4-wheeler, or motorcycle.

She can be reached at ch.richards2010@yahoo.com

Or visit her at www.charlie-richards.com.